"Somebody wants to put me away for murder."

To Abby's horror, tears burned in her eyes. "I didn't do it and I can't just sit around and do nothing while somebody on this ranch comes after me." She swallowed hard, trying to control the tears, but failing. "I've never felt so frightened, or so alone."

Luke pulled her into his arms. For a moment, as tears splashed down her cheeks, she leaned into him. His T-shirt smelled of sunshine and strength, and she allowed herself to be weak, allowed him to hold her up both physically and emotionally.

It felt so good. She felt as if she'd spent her lifetime alone, and in these moments of allowing Luke to support her, she gave him her trust, a tiny piece of her heart.

"Is there anything I can do?" he asked when she finally moved out of his embrace.

She shook her head, then smiled. "You just did it."

Dear Reader,

Take three sisters, a failing ranch, a bevy of bad guys and three strong, handsome cowboys and you have the ingredients for CHEYENNE NIGHTS, my new series for Harlequin Intrigue.

Ranch life in Wyoming takes a special breed of woman. The Connor sisters are that unique breed. They derive their strength from—and share a bond with—each other and their land. The only thing missing in each of their lives is love.

Developing three very special men for the Connor sisters was pure joy. They possess all the qualities I hope the readers will love. I know I adore them.

I hope you enjoy the stories of these strong women as they fight for their home, encounter danger and discover the men who will bring them passion and love on those CHEYENNE NIGHTS.

Happy reading,

Carla Cassidy

Midnight Wishes
Carla Cassidy

Harlequin Books

TORONTO • NEW YORK • LONDON
AMSTERDAM • PARIS • SYDNEY • HAMBURG
STOCKHOLM • ATHENS • TOKYO • MILAN
MADRID • WARSAW • BUDAPEST • AUCKLAND

ISBN 0-373-22415-X

MIDNIGHT WISHES

Copyright © 1997 by Carla Bracale

This edition published by arrangement with Harlequin Books S.A.

® and TM are trademarks of the publisher. Trademarks indicated with
® are registered in the United States Patent and Trademark Office, the
Canadian Trade Marks Office and in other countries.

Printed in U.S.A.

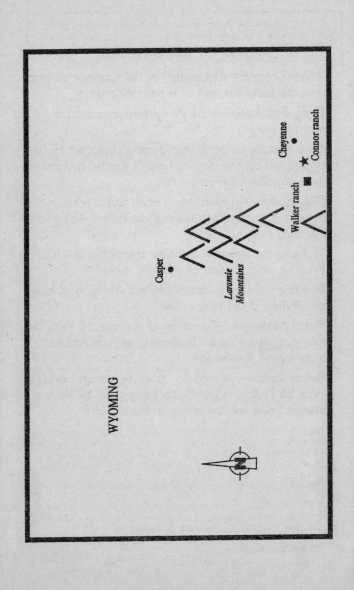

CAST OF CHARACTERS

Abby Connor—The eldest of the Connor sisters and the lead suspect in a murder case.

Greg Foxwood—Abby's ex-husband and a murder victim.

Luke Black—A dark, handsome stranger. He'd appeared on the day of Greg's death, his dark eyes shadowed with secrets.

Billy Sims—An alcoholic ranch hand who nursed a grudge big enough to frame Abby for murder.

Richard Helstrom—The new deputy in town... Was he after justice or Abby's ranch?

Bulldog—In his quest to protect Abby, had he committed a heinous crime?

Rusty Maxwell—Foreman of the ranch. Was he taking care of ranch business, or was Abby truly losing her mind?

Roger Eaton—A smiling, friendly ranch hand. Was he simply a good worker or did he have ulterior motives for being at the ranch?

Prologue

Abby stood beneath the tree, waiting for her sisters to join her. She'd given them the secret code at dinner, knowing by whispering the words "dragon tree," they would understand it was time for a late night meeting.

Moonlight filtered through the leaves of the ancient oak tree, shining silvery shards of light onto the sweet, dew-kissed grass. For as long as Abby could remember, the tree had been referred to as the dragon tree. Their mother had told Abby and her younger sisters that the tree had been struck by lightning dozens of times, resulting in blackened, twisted branches and dense foliage that through the spring and summer grew in the shape of a dragon. In the autumn, the magnificent beast appeared to shed fire-colored scales.

Rather than be frightened, the three girls had embraced the tree, fitting it into their childhood fantasies of princes and castles, of princesses and love.

Abby checked her wristwatch, wondering what was keeping her sisters. Normally whenever the code was given by any one of them, they met at the tree at

eleven. It was a few minutes after that now and there
was no sign of either Colette or Belinda.

Abby thought about sitting down to wait, but was
too wound up and instead paced back and forth beneath the tree. A horse neighed softly from the corral,
and a cow lowed mournfully from the pasture. To
Abby the sounds were as familiar as her father's
voice, as sweet as the lullaby her mother used to sing
to her as a child. She loved the ranch with a fierce-
ness, just as she loved her sisters.

She turned and looked toward the house, seeing
Colette and Belinda running up the hill toward where
Abby awaited. Her heart expanded. At twelve, Colette
was built like a newborn colt, all arms and legs and
breathless impatience. Thirteen-year-old Belinda was
quieter, the most gentle of the three.

"What's going on?" Colette asked as she leaned
against the trunk of the tree.

"Yeah, Abby. What's going on? Why'd you call
us here?" Belinda asked.

Fifteen-year-old Abby sat and wrapped her arms
around her knees. "I found some papers today in
Mom's dresser drawer."

"What kind of papers?" Belinda asked.

Abby looked first at Belinda, then at Colette. She'd
wrestled all afternoon trying to decide if she should
tell her sisters what she'd found. She'd finally decided
they had a right to know. "Adoption papers."

For a moment silence expanded in the air as both
her sisters stared at her. "Adoption papers?" Belinda
finally broke the silence. "Adoption papers for
who?"

"I didn't look. I was looking for Mom's yellow scarf and saw an envelope in her drawer. It was just a manila envelope and written on it was 'adoption papers.' I saw it, then heard Mom coming down the hall so I didn't get a chance to open it. I went back in later to look, but the papers weren't there anymore."

Belinda frowned. "But…but that means one of us must be…"

"No." The word exploded from Colette. "No, I don't want to hear about it, I don't even want to think about it." She leaned forward and reached for Abby's hand, then grabbed Belinda's. "We're sisters. The three of us—and no stupid papers will ever change that."

Abby hadn't realized until that moment there had been a hard ball of fear in her chest. At Colette's words, the ball seeped away and relief flooded her. She'd been afraid, so afraid that they wouldn't feel as strong, as loyal as she did. "Belinda? Do you feel the same way about it?" Abby asked.

Belinda squeezed both her sisters' hands. "Of course. I don't ever want to know which one of us might be in that folder."

Abby withdrew her hands and reached into her pocket. "I was hoping you guys would say that." She pulled out a large safety pin. "I vote we become blood sisters and we vow we'll never try to find out which one of us might be adopted."

As they each pricked their fingers, then pressed them together, again love swelled inside Abby's chest. Even though she was just two years older than

Belinda and three older than Colette, Abby took the role of big sister quite seriously.

"Sisters forever," Abby proclaimed solemnly.

"Sisters forever," Belinda echoed.

"And no matter what happens, we never read those stupid papers," Colette exclaimed. They raised their hands, fingers pressed together, forming a triangle of unity.

With the innocence of youth and the optimism of girlhood, they truly believed it was a vow they could keep. In the distance thunder rumbled, sounding like Fate's laughter as dark clouds moved to steal the moonlight from the sky.

Chapter One

Abby Connor felt his gaze before she actually saw him, a prickling sensation on the nape of her neck as she sat on the porch watching the sunset.

She turned her head first in the direction of the shed, then the barn and there spied him. He stood in the shadows of dusk, his features obscured by the coming darkness of the night. However, the shadows didn't dilute the piercing intensity of his gaze.

Abby had never seen him before. So, who was he and what was he doing here?

Behind her the house radiated an unnatural silence. Everyone had left earlier in the evening to go into town, but Abby had preferred to stay home. She'd intended to get some paperwork done, but had discovered herself too restless to stay cooped up in the office.

She shifted positions on the wicker chair, uncomfortable beneath the cowboy's scrutiny. Something about it made her feel vulnerable, far too alone.

Get a grip, Abby, she admonished herself. After all, she was the boss around here. If she wanted to find out who the unfamiliar cowboy was, all she had to do was ask. She rose, at the same time gesturing to the man.

He ambled toward her with a loose-hipped walk that breathed a combination of sexual suggestion with a hint of confident swagger. He left the shadows of the barn and stepped into the evening light. The shades of sunset stroked his bold, handsome features and stirred an emotion in Abby that had been dormant for a long time.

"Ma'am." He swept the dark hat off his head, revealing midnight-colored hair and eyes the same shade. His face was tanned, his nose straight, his chin square. All the features combined to give him an air of rugged masculinity and quiet strength.

"I haven't seen you around here before."

One corner of his mouth rose sardonically. "I haven't been around before. Your foreman, Rusty, hired me this morning."

Abby flushed, feeling the heat of his gaze as it swept the length of her body. She suddenly wished her shorts weren't so short, or her tank top quite so tight. "What's your name?"

"Luke. Luke Black."

The name suited him, hard and dark.

"And you are?" One sooty eyebrow danced upward.

"Abby. Abby Connor. I run this ranch."

"Ah, you're that one."

Something in his tone rankled Abby. "That one?"

He smiled and again Abby felt the stir of hormones that had been asleep for the past six years. "I heard there are three sisters. One who is married, one who is shy...and the eldest who is boss lady and hates men.''

Abby smiled coolly. ''I don't hate all men, just wise-ass cowboys.'' She waved her hand in dismissal. ''I don't want to keep you from your work.''

He whipped his hat back onto his head, the rakish angle once again hiding his eyes. ''Nice meeting you, Abby. I look forward to working with you.''

She bit the impulse to call after him, to remind him that he worked for her, not with her. Instead she merely watched as he walked away, unable to help but notice the pull of his T-shirt across his broad shoulders, the fit of his jeans against his slender hips and long legs. The man was attractive in a wild, primitive sort of way. She frowned as she noticed the shine of his boots. She'd never seen a ranch hand wearing new boots before.

Definitely attractive...and intriguing. Although brief, his conversation had seemed overlaid with a smooth sensuality. With an irritated sigh, she turned and went into the house. Okay, so he was sexy and handsome and she'd just proven to herself that she was divorced, not dead. Despite her resolve to never marry again, never give her heart away, she could still appreciate a fine-looking man.

The ranch house surrounded her with its quiet and for a moment Abby was sorry she hadn't gone with her family into town. She wandered into her son's room, her gaze immediately captured by the items on his dressertop. Rocks, old bird nests, seed pods and a variety of nature's gifts nearly hid the oak wood. She shook her head and smiled. At six years old, Cody would be thrilled if he could bring all of the outside in.

She left his room and went into the kitchen. Stealing a glance into the refrigerator, seeking a snack, she realized what she really wanted was a piece of apple pie. Unfortunately, Maria, their cook, hadn't baked for several days.

"No problem," Abby said to herself as she hurried to her bedroom. She changed into a pair of jeans and a light cotton blouse, then grabbed her truck keys. Nobody had better pie than the Great Day Diner. With a fifteen minute drive she could have her pie and enjoy the conversation of neighbors. She scribbled a quick note to her family, in case they got home before her, then left the house.

As she walked out into the twilight there was no sign of the disturbing cowboy. She felt relieved, yet oddly disappointed. Shoving thoughts of him aside, she got into the truck and started the engine.

As she drove, she tried to keep her thoughts off unpleasant things. She didn't want to think about the fact that the ranch was in bad financial straits and the Connor sisters might not be able to hang on to their home for much longer.

She definitely didn't want to think about the fact that her ex-husband had been in town for the past week.

She tightened her grip on the steering wheel and instead focused on the landscape. As far as she was concerned there was no place more beautiful than the area in and around Cheyenne, Wyoming. The towering mountains, the valleys of green pastures and the terra-cotta colored buttes rising above like ancient sentries guarding all. There was a sense of enduring strength, and Abby knew much of her own inner strength came from the land.

Wheeling into the diner parking lot, she tried not to worry about the future of the Connor ranch, telling herself somehow, someway it would be all right. As far as Greg...hopefully he'd go back to where he'd come from and leave her and Cody alone.

The interior of the diner embraced her like an old friend. Cool air, rich cooking scents, and friendly waves from neighbors and acquaintances made her worries fall away. Known for the endless supply of good coffee and baked goods, the diner on the outskirts of Cheyenne was a popular place for people to spend the end of their day.

Abby slid into one of the red vinyl booths and smiled as the waitress approached, coffeepot in hand. "Hi, Sheila."

"Hey, Abby, where's that handsome cowboy sidekick of yours?"

For a brief moment a vision of the sexy Luke Black filled Abby's mind. She blinked away the image and realized Sheila was talking about Cody. "He went with his aunts and uncle into town for a movie. How's your dad? He hasn't been out to the ranch in a while."

Sheila grinned. "You know Dad. He's keeping the prairies safe for women and children everywhere. I'll tell him you asked about him."

"You do that." Pleasure swept through Abby at

thoughts of the big, burly sheriff who'd been like a surrogate father to the Connor sisters.

"What can I get for you?" Sheila asked as she splashed coffee into Abby's cup.

"A piece of apple pie and the coffee should do it."

"Back in a jiffy." Sheila left to grab a piece of pie, then returned, sliding the generous slice toward Abby as she sat opposite her in the booth. "So, give me some good gossip. Things have been far too quiet and boring around here lately."

Abby laughed. "Who has time to hear gossip? Keeping our heads above water at the ranch takes all my time and energy."

"Colette and that handsome husband of hers come in regularly with that sweet little girl of theirs. I wonder if the two of them will ever stop acting like newlyweds."

Abby smiled at thoughts of her younger sister and Hank, the man she'd married. "It's only been a month since the wedding, they're still allowed to act like newlyweds. Now, if I can just find a good man for Belinda."

Sheila frowned. "Didn't she used to date Derek Walker before he left town?"

Abby nodded. "I think Derek was Belinda's first real love." She frowned and took a bite of the pie, not wanting to think about the man who had been her first love.

"Speaking of first loves...your ex has been in and out of here during the last week," Sheila said, as if plucking the thought straight out of Abby's head.

"Yes, I heard he's back in town. I'm hoping if I ignore him he'll go away."

"Speak of the devil..." Sheila gestured to the diner door, where Greg Foxwood had just walked in. "I don't think you're going to be able to ignore him this time." Sheila stood as Greg approached their booth.

"Sheila." Greg nodded, a slow smile stretching across his handsome face. "How's the prettiest little waitress in town?"

Sheila's face blushed a becoming pale pink. "I'm fine, you scamp."

"Why don't you bring me a cup of coffee?" He slid into the seat Sheila had vacated. "I need to have a little chat with my ex-wife."

As Sheila left, Abby fought the impulse to get up and leave. She'd successfully managed to avoid Greg for the past week, but she'd known all along a confrontation was inevitable.

For a long moment she simply stared at the man she'd once loved with all the passion of a teenage girl. He'd changed little in the past six years. His hair was still a luxurious black, his blue eyes as clear as a spring Wyoming sky.

With the wisdom of years and the objectivity of heartbreak, she also noticed more telling features. A weak chin she knew indicated his lack of character, thin lips that hinted at a hidden cruelty.

She searched her heart, seeking some remnant of love for the man who'd fathered Cody. There was none. "What do you want, Greg?"

He laced his hands on the tabletop and bent toward her. "You know what I want."

"Let me guess. Money."

He leaned back against the red vinyl and eyed her lazily. "Nope. You aren't going to buy me off this time."

She quirked an eyebrow. "Why not? Don't tell me you've actually managed to acquire some character."

"Oh, Abby, you wound me." He paused as Sheila reappeared at the table and poured his coffee. When Sheila left once again, Greg looked at Abby, his eyes hard and cold. "I want a relationship with my son."

Abby balled her hands in her lap. "That's rich," she said bitterly. "Especially coming from a man who walked out when Cody was mere weeks old."

"I did the right thing. I married you, didn't I? I gave the kid my name."

Abby stared at him incredulously. Did he really believe that's all she'd needed from him, a cheap diamond ring and his last name? "The right thing? You deserted us." She drew a deep breath to steady herself. "Greg, if you really want to do the right thing for Cody, you won't see him. You've disappointed him so many times in the past with your letters filled with empty promises."

"He's my kid just as much as he's yours. I got rights."

"Your rights were terminated when you walked out on us." Abby flushed, realizing she'd shouted the words and had garnered the attention of the people around them. Again she took a deep breath. "Greg, Cody is a happy, well-adjusted little boy. If you really love him, if you really care about him, leave him be."

"A boy needs a father."

"A boy needs a role model and you aren't the one I want Cody to have. Twice before you've chosen money over seeing your son. That tells me all I need to know."

"All that tells you is that I was temporarily low on funds." He sipped his coffee, apparently unaffected by the turmoil he created in her. "Aren't you going to finish your pie?" he asked.

She shook her head. Her guts were too twisted with emotion to eat. She should have left the moment he walked through the door. "How long are you in town for?" she asked. "A day…another week? How can you possibly be a positive part of Cody's life when you can't get your own life together?"

"Maybe when I leave this time I'll just take the kid with me, teach him a little about real life."

His words sent a cold fear shimmying up Abby's spine. The fear was quickly usurped by rage…a rage that nearly blinded her as she slid out of the booth.

She leaned toward him, uncaring who heard her, what disruption she caused. "Listen to me, Greg, and listen well. I'm warning you right now. Stay away from Cody." She strode toward the door, then turned to him again. "You hear me? You try in any way to take Cody from me, you mess with our lives in any way—and I'll kill you. I'll kill you."

She slammed out of the diner and toward her truck, her anger still trembling through her. Damn him. Damn his black soul. She got into the truck and leaned her forehead against the steering wheel, trying to get her tumultuous emotions under control.

Slowly her anger ebbed, leaving behind only a hollow ache of despair. She started the truck and took off, knowing she couldn't go home just yet. She didn't want Cody or the rest of her family to see her so emotionally distraught.

She drove aimlessly, the window down to allow in the warm night air. If she knew for certain that Greg truly wanted to be a father to Cody, she wouldn't stop him. But leopards didn't change their spots.

Greg had proven to her over and over again that his reasons for wanting to see Cody were less than altruistic. Twice before Greg had contacted Abby about seeing Cody, both times hinting broadly that for a little cold cash he'd go away. She'd paid him and he'd disappeared.

This time was different. He was here in Cheyenne and threatening to take Cody. His game had suddenly changed and she didn't know the rules. She tightened her hands on the steering wheel.

Greg had stolen her dreams years ago, seduced away her innocence, but she'd be damned if he'd steal her son. She'd see him in hell first.

LUKE BLACK SAT on the bed he'd been assigned in the bunkhouse and eased off his cowboy boots. He closed his eyes and rubbed a foot, wondering if another day in the damned boots would permanently cripple him. How in the hell did the other men wear boots day in and day out?

The bunkhouse reminded Luke of his army days. Although it was too dark to make out the other beds in the room, a variety of snores and grunts attested to the fact that they were filled with ranch hands. Most of them had been smart enough to go to bed at a reasonable hour, knowing daybreak and work came early. But then, most of them didn't have any personal interest in Miss Abby Connor.

In his stocking feet, using the moonlight as his guide, he walked over to the window that looked out onto the ranch house. Several hours ago a carload of people had come home, but Abby hadn't returned. He eyed the luminous hands on his wristwatch. Two o'clock.

Where had she gone? He'd seen her drive away hours ago. Did she have a lover? Somehow he didn't think so. When he'd spoken to her earlier, he'd noted an untouchable quality in her eyes, a cool distance that made him believe it had been a long time since she'd been touched by passion.

He limped back to his bed and eased down, grateful that the mattress was soft and accommodating. Life as a ranch hand wasn't as easy as he'd anticipated. But then, when had life ever been easy for him?

Still, the physical labor felt good. He'd spent too many years cooped up in his accounting office, depending on hours at the gym to keep him in shape.

Throwing an arm across his eyes, he thought of Abby Connor. She hadn't been what he'd expected, although he wasn't exactly sure what he'd been expecting. He only knew he hadn't foreseen the pale wheat color of her short hair, nor the unruly curls that danced like a frame around her face. She'd worn no makeup, but hadn't needed any to emphasize the blue of her eyes. He had anticipated she'd be attractive, but hadn't been prepared for her fresh-eyed, unspoiled prettiness.

He wasn't fooled. She might look like a long-legged, milk-complected ranch girl, but he knew her heart was black. He wondered if Abby Connor had any idea just how difficult her life was about to get.

DESPITE THE FACT that it had been nearly three when she'd finally gotten home the night before, Abby awoke at dawn. The first thing she did was go into Cody's room.

Standing over him as he slept, her heart expanded with the kind of love she knew she'd never feel for another human being. Fierce, so intense it stole her breath away, her love for Cody was the sweetest, most pure of emotions.

Gently she wiped an errant strand of pale hair from his forehead, breathing in the sweet scent of childhood. One thing Abby had to give Greg...he'd made a beautiful son. And if she knew Greg would be a healthy presence in Cody's life, she'd accommodate his wish to see his son. She leaned down and kissed Cody's forehead, smiling as he puckered a frown.

Belting her robe around her waist, she left his room and padded to the kitchen. For a moment she wondered why Maria hadn't started coffee yet, then remembered that today was the cook's day off.

The fight the night before with Greg had left a bitter aftertaste in her mouth. She started to make coffee, then decided instead to treat herself to a cup of her favorite hot chocolate mix.

It took her only minutes to heat the water in the

microwave, then scoop two teaspoonfuls of the mix from the canister where she kept the special mixture.

She sat at the table and wrapped her hands around the warm mug. Her sisters teased her about her being the only woman in the world who drank hot chocolate year-round.

She took a sip, enjoying the rich chocolate taste with the hint of raspberry sweetness. The concoction was made especially for her in a specialty shop in Cheyenne.

Her thoughts turned back to her conversation with Greg. Was he bluffing? Was this just another attempt to extort more money from her, or was he really serious about trying to take Cody? Lord knew she didn't have the money for a custody battle.

It was hard to believe she'd once thought herself so in love with Greg Foxwood. She'd just turned eighteen when he'd drifted into town and come to work on the Connor ranch. Instantly she'd developed a crush on the flirting, handsome man. She realized now he'd taken advantage of her youth and inexperience. They'd made love in the moonlight half a dozen times before she'd discovered herself pregnant.

"Moonlight madness," she said aloud with a frown. "Or temporary insanity." Somehow she thought it was more the latter than the former.

While she was thrilled that Colette had found and married the prince of her dreams, and she desperately hoped Belinda would someday find a special man, Abby had long ago set aside her dreams of love and happily-ever-after.

Luke Black was wrong. She didn't hate men. She

just didn't have any dreams left to share with a man.
She was a single mother running a failing ranch. She
didn't have the time or energy for a relationship.

With a disgusted sigh, she emptied her mind of
nonsense and instead focused on making a pot of coffee in anticipation of the others soon getting up for a
new day.

Dawn was just chasing away the last of the night
clouds when a knock resounded on the back door.
Frowning, wondering who would be here so early, she
hurried to answer.

"Can I come in for a minute?"

Abby eyed Sheriff Junior Blanchard in surprise.
"It's awfully early for a social call, Junior," she said
as she opened the screen door to allow him in.

"This isn't a social call."

A flutter of anxiety rippled through Abby's stomach as Junior's stern features didn't relax into his
usual friendly smile. "Hmm, sounds ominous. Come
on in. I just made a fresh pot of coffee."

She pointed him to a chair at the large oak table,
then poured two cups of coffee and joined him. "So,
what has you out here so early? And without a smile?
Did I forget to pay some traffic tickets or something?" She grinned, the smile slowly fading when
Junior didn't return it. "Junior, what's wrong?"

The sheriff passed a hand through his thick gray
hair, his gaze not quite meeting hers. "Abby, I've got
some bad news. Greg is dead."

Abby hissed inwardly in shock. "Dead?" Her head
reeled as she stared at Junior in horror. "How...
when?"

"He was murdered, Abby."

"Oh, my God." Immediately all kinds of mental images filled her head. She'd hoped, she'd prayed, for many things where Greg was concerned, but she'd never wanted him dead. Now there would be no opportunities for Greg to mature and become the father Cody needed. She looked at Junior, still stunned by the news.

"Somebody took a branding iron and hit him over the head. The branding iron was from this ranch. It happened between the hours of ten and two." Junior's gaze held weariness, sympathy and something else…something that caused another shiver of apprehension to sweep through Abby. "Abby, I need to know where you were in the hours between ten o'clock last night and two o'clock this morning."

Abby stared at him, suddenly recognizing the alien emotion she saw in his eyes. Suspicion. Heaven help her, Junior thought she'd murdered Greg.

Chapter Two

Abby stared at Junior in horror. "Junior, you can't actually believe I had anything to do with Greg's death."

"It doesn't much matter what I believe. I've got to follow leads and facts, and facts are, I've got a dozen people who heard you threaten Greg last night hours before he was found dead." Junior shoved his coffee cup aside as if he'd lost any taste for the brew.

A vision of herself leaving the diner, spewing threats, filled Abby's mind. She'd been so angry, so frightened. She didn't even remember everything she'd said, but she did remember telling Greg she'd kill him. Stupid, empty threats, that's all they'd been. "Junior, you know I could never hurt anyone," she exclaimed. "You've known me all my life. You know what kind of person I am."

"I know how much you love that boy of yours, and I figure you never know what a person is capable of when they're pushed into a corner." Again his gaze didn't quite meet hers. "Abby, now's the time to talk. You know I'll do what I can to help you, but I can't help if you don't tell me the truth."

"Junior." Abby reached out and took his big, gnarled hand in hers. "I'm telling you the truth. I had nothing to do with Greg's death."

His hand squeezed hers and his eyes flashed with paternal tenderness. "I've got to tell you, Abby girl, right now it doesn't look good." He gave her hand a final squeeze, then released it. "Of course, the investigation has just begun. Now..." He took a notepad from his breast pocket and flipped it open, then withdrew a pen. "Tell me where you were last night between the hours of ten and two."

Abby sighed, knowing he wasn't going to like her answer. "After I left the diner, I was so angry—too angry to go home. So I drove for a while. I finally ended up at Walker's pond. I must have fallen asleep, because before I knew it, it was about a quarter to three and I drove home."

Junior winced. "Walker's pond, huh. I don't suppose you saw anyone, spoke to anybody who can corroborate your whereabouts?"

"Walker's pond isn't exactly Main Street," she replied dryly. The pond was part of the Walker place whose land abutted the Connor ranch. The Walker house had burned down three years before and the Walker family had moved away. "There was nobody else around while I was there."

"What about on the way? Did you pass anyone who might remember your truck heading in that direction?"

Abby felt as if she'd been plunged into a nightmare. Greg's death felt unreal and she knew it would take time for the actuality to sink in. She rubbed her forehead, concentrating on Junior's question. "No. I don't remember passing anyone or anyone passing me." She looked at the man who'd been like a father to her since her parents' death. "Junior, am I going to be arrested?"

"Abby girl, I can't answer that. There just isn't enough information yet. But I'm not going to lie to you. It doesn't look good." He stood and walked toward the back door. "Did Greg have any family? We don't know who to notify as next of kin."

Abby frowned thoughtfully. "I know his parents died when he was a teenager. Other than mentioning that, Greg rarely spoke about any family. He always talked like he was a drifter, with no ties anywhere."

Junior nodded. "I'll be in touch." He started out the door, then turned back to her. "I know you've heard it in the movies before, but I'd advise you not to leave town right now." With those ominous words, he left.

Abby remained at the table, her mind whirling in a fog of disbelief. Greg was dead, and from what Junior had implied, she was the number one suspect.

"Good mornin'." Belinda came into the kitchen, still looking half asleep. Her dark blond hair was captured in an untidy braid at the back of her neck and her eyes held the glaze of lingering sleep.

"No, it's not a good morning," Abby replied. "Greg was murdered last night."

Belinda gasped, her eyes losing the remnants of any sleepiness. "What?"

"He was hit over the head with one of our branding irons. Junior just left a few minutes ago." Abby realized she didn't even know where the murder had taken place. She'd been too shocked, both by the murder and by Junior's suspicions, to ask any pertinent questions. "I don't know much more, other than he's dead and I'm the prime suspect."

"Oh, Abby." Belinda sank into the chair opposite her older sister. She took Abby's hands in hers. "I'm so sorry for you. Even though you and Greg were divorced, this loss must hurt."

Abby looked at her in surprise. Loss? She was sorry Greg was dead, horrified that somebody had taken his life, but as she searched her heart, she felt no loss. "I lost Greg years ago. I grieved for him when he left us. I feel guilty now because I've got no grief left."

Belinda nodded, apparently remembering the grieving process Abby had gone through when Greg had walked out on her years before. "Why would you be considered a leading suspect? How can Junior even think such a thing? That's the most ridiculous thing I've ever heard."

"Not so ridiculous," Abby returned. She quickly told her sister about meeting Greg in the diner and the threats she'd shouted as she'd slammed out into the night. "How was I to know hours later somebody would kill him and my stupid threats would come back to haunt me?"

Belinda released Abby's hands and smiled reassuringly. "I'm sure it will all be fine. Surely nobody in their right mind could really believe you killed Greg." She stood and poured herself a cup of coffee, then sat once again. "Maybe Colette and Hank should cancel their plans to leave town this weekend."

"No. I don't want them to do that. They've had their trip to Las Vegas planned for the last month." Abby thought of her youngest sister and her husband. They'd gotten married a month before, but hadn't had a chance for a honeymoon. "They've already got their plane tickets and hotel reservations, and the baby is finally over her ear infection."

"You know they wouldn't mind postponing their trip."

"I know. But there's nothing they can do for Greg or for me by staying here. It's better they go."

A knock fell on the back door and both women jumped. "What now?" Abby murmured, then relaxed slightly as Rusty Maxwell, the ranch foreman, stepped inside.

"Miss Abby, I saw Junior before he left, he told me about Mr. Foxwood's death." The old man worried the rim of his dusty brown hat between his workworn fingers. "I'm sorry about your loss and I hate to bother you, but I need a check. I've got the supplies coming for that new fence in the south pasture."

"I'm going to the barn," Belinda said as she placed her cup in the sink. With a wave of one hand, she disappeared out the door.

Abby turned to her foreman and frowned. "New fence?"

Rusty nodded. "We talked about it last week."

Abby rubbed her forehead, her thoughts scattered like windblown seeds. "I thought we just bought fencing supplies."

"We did, for the north pasture." Rusty rubbed his gray whisker-stubbled chin thoughtfully. "If it's a problem, I suppose we can mend it one more time, but sooner or later we're going to have to buy new."

"No. We might as well do it right now. I'll be back." Abby left the kitchen and went down the hallway to the ranch office.

As always, when she entered the small room, a vision of her father bloomed in her head. Before his death, he'd spent long hours in this room, smoking his pipe, dreaming about being a prosperous rancher. Unfortunately, he'd been better at dreaming of making money than actually accomplishing it.

When the elder Connors had died in a car accident, they'd left behind their three daughters and a ranch teetering on the edge of financial ruin. The sisters' attempt to save the ranch by renovating several buildings and turning it into a kind of dude ranch had so far been unsuccessful. The guests were few and far between and finances hadn't improved.

Abby walked over to the desk and pulled out the checkbook. She tore out a check then lingered for just a moment by the rich walnut desk. The room still retained the faint scent of cherry tobacco and the dreams of a man who'd loved the ranch and had instilled that fierce love in his eldest daughter.

With a sigh of despair, she left the room and hurried back to the kitchen where Rusty waited. "I met our newest ranch hand yesterday," she said as she handed him the check.

"Luke? Yeah, he showed up yesterday morning looking for work. Since Hank is leaving this weekend, we need the extra hands. I don't know how long he'll stick around, but we can use him as long as he's here.''

Abby remembered the shiny boots the man had worn. Odd. "What do you know about him?"

Rusty flashed her a smile. "You know me, Miss Abby, all I care about is that the men are good workers. Don't care much about their past or future as long as their shoulders are broad and their arms strong."

Luke Black's shoulders had definitely been broad. She shoved aside thoughts of the disturbing, attractive man and focused on the gray-haired cowboy in front of her.

"Rusty, things might get a little difficult around here for a while. I'll be honest with you, I don't know how Greg's death will affect everything. Right now what evidence Junior has gathered points to me having had something to do with the murder."

Her throat tightened with the words. "If I'm charged, I'm going to be depending on you to see that things run smoothly here while I go through a trial." The very thought was almost overwhelming.

Rusty reached out and patted her shoulder. "Don't you worry none, Miss Abby. I've been working this ranch for the last fifteen years, I ain't about to let things go."

Abby wrapped her arms around herself, fighting a chill. "The vultures are circling. You've probably heard I've had two offers on the ranch in the last couple of weeks."

Rusty nodded. "I heard. A man don't burp that folks around here don't talk about it."

"Both Henry Carsworth and Deputy Helstrom have made me offers."

"Carsworth is a city slicker who doesn't know the front end of a horse from the back," Rusty snorted.

"Needless to say, I turned both offers down." Again Abby fought off a shiver. "I guess we'll just have to wait and see what the next couple of weeks bring."

Rusty held up the check. "Guess I'd better get back to work."

She nodded, her thoughts jumping from one subject to another. The morning already seemed overwhelming and she fought the impulse to jump back into bed and pull the blankets over her head.

"Mornin', Mom. What's for breakfast? I'm starving."

Dread rolled around in her stomach as Abby turned and faced her son. His pale blond hair spiked out like sprouting wheat and when he smiled, his lips parted to expose a missing front tooth. Clad in a pair of pajamas decorated with horses and spurs, his face radiated sleepy innocence.

Abby's heart fell deeper into her chest as she realized the difficulty of her morning wasn't over yet. She hadn't even fully absorbed the emotional shock of Greg's death herself and she now had to face the discomfiting task of telling her son his father had been killed. "Sit down, honey. I've got something I have to tell you."

THE EARLY MORNING sun splashed warmth on Abby's back as she made her way to the stable. There was a slight breeze, reminiscent of the lingering of spring in the air, and the scent of hay, sweet grass and wild-flowers embraced her. A perfect morning for a ride on Blackheart.

It wasn't often Cody slept in and Maria offered to keep the boy inside while Abby enjoyed an early morning ride. Abby intended to take advantage of the time alone and ride out to where the workers were putting in the new fence.

The horse greeted her before she saw him, nick-ering pleasure as Abby entered the stable. Abby smiled as she approached the last stall, where the black quarter horse, already saddled, awaited her.

Blackheart had been a gift from a neighbor and had earned his name while Abby's brother-in-law, Hank, had trained him. Many mornings Abby was pulled from her work by Hank's shouts as the horse threw him again and again. "You black-hearted creature," Hank would exclaim as he dusted off his backside.

"Come on, sweetie," Abby said as she led the magnificent beast from the stall. As they walked out-side, Blackheart danced with high spirits, as if antic-ipating a run.

With the ease of habit, Abby swung herself up and onto Blackheart's back. Grasping the reins, she set off at a pleasant gait.

It had been three days since Greg's murder. No-body from the sheriff's department had been out to question her again. In an ironic twist, as Greg's only known kin, Abby had made the arrangements for the funeral that would take place tomorrow. Greg would be buried in the Connor family plot with Abby's parents.

She shoved thoughts of funerals and death aside, needing this moment to just breathe in the sweet, scented air, revel in the beauty of the morning. Time enough for reality later.

She gave Blackheart his head, allowing him to pick up speed as they raced across the fields toward the south. Abby's body automatically adjusted to the rhythm of the run, molding to the horse as if they were one entity.

The wind rippled through her hair and stung her cheeks, but she didn't rein in. Instead she reveled in the wildness of the run. It was impossible to focus on any problems with the power and speed of Blackheart beneath her.

Connor land flashed by her, filling her heart with both pride and despair. She couldn't lose the ranch. She just couldn't. Somehow, she'd find a way to hang on.

It wasn't until she saw the ranch hands in the distance by the fence line that she reined in and slowed the horse to a walk.

One particular cowboy caught and held her attention. Luke Black. She hadn't seen him since that first meeting on the evening of Greg's murder. Again she felt a shock of pleasure race through her at his physical attractiveness.

His bare chest gleamed with a coating of perspiration, delineating each muscle mass as he swung a sledgehammer up over his head, then brought it down on a post. Each blow drove the post deeper and deeper into the ground.

Dark hair formed a valentine design on his chest, the tail of the heart elongated, creeping down his stomach and disappearing into the jeans that rode low on his hips.

A coil of heat unfurled in Abby's stomach and swept through her with provocative intensity. Something about Luke Black affected her in a visceral way.

He paused in his labor, as if he felt her gaze, and turned toward her. The rim of his dusty hat hid his eyes from her view. He released his hold on the sledgehammer and allowed it to fall to the ground with a thud. "Morning, Abby."

Her name on his lips had a smooth familiarity that instantly put her back up. "Luke." She nodded curtly.

He swept his hat off his head, exposing his rich dark hair to the gleam of the sun. He pulled a bandanna from his jeans pocket and wiped it across his forehead. "Nice horse," he observed.

"Thanks. He's my favorite." She leaned over and patted the horse's neck. "His name is Blackheart."

Something in Luke's eyes flickered, an inner amusement along with a tightening of his jaw. "Nice piece of flesh," he added, his gaze not on the horse but rather skimming the thin fabric of her blouse.

Abby felt a flame of heat sweep up her neck and suffuse her face. Damn the man, he seemed to have the ability to make her feel quite naked. She felt like Lady Godiva without her curtain of hair.

She dismounted the horse and surveyed the broken

fence line and the ranch hands still working. "What do you think, another day or two and it will be finished?"

He nodded. "We should be able to get it finished by tomorrow night." He moved the bandanna down his neck, blotting at the hollow of his throat where a pulse pounded visibly. "Heard about your husband's death."

"Ex-husband."

"Whatever." His eyes glittered darkly. "I must say, you seem to be taking it all very well. Mourning becomes you."

Abby stiffened, recognizing a vague censure in his tone. "I don't think you know me well enough to understand how I'm handling anything."

"Then have dinner with me tonight and let me get to know you better."

Abby stared at him, shocked. Her stomach fluttered as she thought of spending any length of time alone with Luke and his dark eyes and suggestive smile. She caressed Blackheart's muzzle, trying to ignore the butterflies inside her. "I'm afraid that's impossible. I have a rule and never get personally involved with the men who work for me."

He wiped the bandanna across the width of his muscled chest. Abby watched the action, wondering if the hair there was soft like fur or coarse and springy. "Then I quit. Now, have dinner with me."

Abby stared at him and a small laugh bubbled out of her. "You can't quit," she protested. "Rusty needs you. The ranch needs you."

"Then break your rule." Although he said the

words lightly, there was an undertone of command that caused Abby to stiffen in defense.

"I don't break rules."

He smiled, a small lifting of the corners of his mouth that did nothing to dispel the intensity of his gaze. "That's not what I heard."

"Oh, really? And what have you heard?"

He took a few more steps toward her, bringing with him the scent of dust, sweat and an underlying tinge of minty soap. It was a distinctively male smell that called to the core of femininity inside her. She took a step backward, bumping into Blackheart's solid side.

"I heard from all the folks in town that when you tire of a man in your life, you just hit him over the head with a branding iron."

Anger surged inside Abby. So, the locals were feeding off this latest tragedy and apparently she was the grist for their rumor mill. She eyed Luke with an eyebrow raised. "If you believe that, then I would think the last woman you'd want to have dinner with would be me. What if I suddenly tire of you?"

His eyes flashed and his grin widened. "I'll take my chances. Besides, I like my women dangerous."

Abby mounted Blackheart, her heart pounding in a foreign rhythm. "If you want to see a dangerous woman, don't give me a good day's work for your pay. That makes me dangerous. Good day, Luke." She turned Blackheart and took off in the direction she'd come.

LUKE WATCHED HER RIDE, unable to help but admire the picture she made on the back of the horse. Her pale blond hair was in sharp contrast to the ebony darkness of the animal. She looked tiny on Blackheart's back, yet completely in control. Blackheart. Ironic that her horse was named the very nickname he'd given her.

"She's a looker, isn't she?"

Luke turned to see Roger Eaton grinning at him. The thin, wiry man leaned on the handle of his shovel, his fair hair shimmering in the sunlight. "You don't stand a chance with her. She's got the coldest heart in the state of Wyoming."

"So I've heard," Luke answered, his gaze going back to where nothing remained of her presence but dust devils stirred by Blackheart's hooves. His eyes narrowed as he thought of the blue of her eyes, the soft curve of her breast against her cotton blouse. The fact that she was attractive only made his mission more pleasant.

"You should have seen her a couple of months ago, when Colette got herself into some trouble. Abby was like a tigress, all teeth and claws."

Colette. Luke knew she was the youngest, the one who'd recently gotten married. "What kind of trouble was Colette in?"

Roger wiped an arm across his forehead. "I don't know the whole story. All I know for sure is she showed up here on the ranch ready to give birth and without a memory in her head. Seems she was a government witness against some powerful lawyer back in California. It all worked out all right and she married the man who was supposed to be protecting her. Anyway, all I know is that Abby loves three things…her two sisters and that kid of hers. Beyond that, the woman has stone where a heart should be."

Luke flashed the young cowboy a quick grin. "I always did like a challenge."

Roger snorted. "I'm just offering some friendly advice. Don't waste your time."

"I figure all I've got to lose is time." Luke tucked his bandanna into his jeans pocket, then picked up his sledgehammer, indicating as far as he was concerned the conversation was over.

What Roger Eaton didn't know—couldn't know— was that Abby Connor was his whole reason for being here. He intended to get to know her, wanted to learn her strengths and weaknesses, her hopes and dreams. Then, systematically, he intended to use that knowledge to destroy her.

Chapter Three

The day was far too beautiful for a funeral. It was as if nature itself mocked the very gravity of the ceremony taking place. Birds called cheerfully and the horses danced and neighed spiritedly in the distant corral.

Weddings and funerals always commanded a crowd and today was no different. Abby guessed between forty and fifty people stood beneath the grove of trees that sheltered the Connor family cemetery.

Abby suspected most people had come less to pay their respects for Greg's passing and more to assuage their curiosity about her...the suspect in Greg's murder case.

Although murder might happen occasionally in the city of Cheyenne, it was rare on the ranches surrounding Cheyenne.

"You all right?" Colette whispered next to her as Preacher Thompson droned on and on. Colette's hand clasped around Abby's arm, supportive and loving.

Abby nodded, wishing she could squeeze out a few tears to satisfy everyone. She had a feeling most of the attendees were holding their breath, hoping she'd throw herself onto the casket and sob out her guilt.

But her eyes remained dry, although her heart entertained a small ache for what might have been had Greg been a different kind of man.

When she'd met him she'd dreamed of what their lives would be like together. They had been sweet, midnight dreams of love and laughter.

She placed a hand on Cody's shoulder. He looked up at her, flashing her a small smile. Greg's death was no more than a stranger's passing to the little boy. He'd been so young when Greg had left; he couldn't grieve for a man he'd never known.

Wishing this were finished, dreading the gathering at the house that would immediately follow, Abby looked around the group of people. Junior Blanchard and Deputy Helstrom stood off to one side, eyeing each and every person as if seeking answers to unspoken questions.

Several of the ranch hands looked ill at ease, their hats in their hands. Abby knew they'd much rather be out working, but she'd called off all work at the ranch for the day.

Her gaze locked with Luke's. His eyes held a stark, naked emotion that for a moment threatened to buckle Abby's knees. Grief. Deep and dark, it flowed from him for just a moment, then was replaced by a knowing smile, making her wonder if she'd seen grief at all.

A shiver raked up her spine as she tried to figure out exactly what she'd seen. Why would Luke Black feel anything about Greg's death? Or had she only imagined that stark moment of grief?

She broke the gaze and instead focused on Preacher Thompson, who with thunder and damnation reverberating in his voice, seemed to be winding down.

With the official ceremony over, the crowd of people began to disperse, although Abby knew over the next several hours most of them would make their way to the main house.

As a unit, the Connors walked the distance back to the house. "Abby, Colette and I don't have to take off tomorrow," Hank said as he shifted Brook, his daughter, from one arm to the other.

"I don't want to hear another word about it," Abby said firmly. "You and Colette and the baby are getting on that plane tomorrow." She smiled at her brother-in-law. "Really, Hank, I insist. There's absolutely nothing you can do here. In fact, if I know you and Colette are having a good time, it will make things easier for me."

"And it's not like she'll be here all alone," Belinda added. "I'll be here with her."

"And me," Cody quipped, not wanting to be left out.

"Besides," Abby continued. "I'm sure it's just a matter of time before Junior and Deputy Helstrom find the person who killed Greg." She hoped her voice rang with more optimism than she felt.

At the house, Maria had prepared for the onslaught of people, a sturdy twenty-cup coffeemaker perked in the kitchen and pitchers of ice tea had been made. Throwaway cups and napkins lined the kitchen table along with several platters of cookies. Abby knew most of the people coming would bring food, as if hot casseroles and baked hams could be a panacea for sorrow.

Abby went to her room to change into cooler, more comfortable clothes and instructed Cody to get out of his little suit and into jeans. She knew better than to expect Cody to keep his suit clean for an entire afternoon.

By the time she returned to the living room, people had begun to arrive.

As with most social gatherings, it didn't take long for the men and women to find different areas of comfort. The women bustled in the kitchen, helping Maria cope with the steady influx of food, and the men rambled out to sit on the porch or lean against the front fence.

Abby drifted back and forth, accepting condolences and trying to ignore the frank stares and whispers that followed in her wake.

"Heard she said she'd kill him..."

"She's always been a cold one..."

"Such a flirt, it's no wonder she killed him..."

The whispers followed her like shadows, snippets of conversations she knew dwelled on everything from speculation on her love life with Greg, to how she might have gotten into his rented room to kill him.

"Abby." Sheila swept her into a friendly embrace. "How you doing, hon?" She pulled Abby out of the living room and into the quiet of the hallway. "I can't believe you got stuck paying for Greg's funeral expenses after all that man didn't do for you.''

Abby smiled. "It seems even in death, Greg is still sucking money from me. But I couldn't just let him be unclaimed, buried in some county plot. As Cody's father, I owe him this much.''

Sheila frowned. "Abby, I'm sorry about having to tell Dad about the fight you and Greg had in the diner on the night he was killed. I hope...I hope you aren't mad at me.''

Abby gripped her friend's hand. "Don't be silly. If you hadn't told your father, somebody else who was in the diner that night would have. Besides, I just had a fight with Greg. I didn't kill him.''

Sheila nodded. "I know that, and so does Dad. But I think he's going to hand over the investigation of the case to Richard.''

"Deputy Helstrom? But why would Junior do that?''

"Dad says he's too close to you. That if he's in charge, people might say he's letting his personal feelings for you get in the way of his job.''

Abby raked a hand through her hair, unhappy at this turn of events. "I'd say Richard Helstrom might be accused of the same thing.''

Sheila frowned. "What do you mean?''

Abby shrugged. "Deputy Helstrom made me an offer on the ranch a couple weeks ago. What better way to tip the scales in favor of me selling to him than by putting me behind bars where I can't hold on to the ranch.''

"Richard would never do a thing like that," Sheila

protested. Abby looked at her, surprised at the vehemence in her defense of the lawman. Sheila blushed prettily. "In the last couple of months since Richard moved to town, we've been seeing each other quite a bit. I know you aren't happy that he wants to buy your ranch, but he really is a nice man."

Abby smiled. "I'm sure you're right. I'd just feel better if Junior remained in charge of finding out who killed Greg." At least she knew Junior would have her best interests at heart. She wasn't so sure about Deputy Richard Helstrom.

"Don't worry, everything is going to be fine," Sheila assured her. "Richard is a good man and he'll work every bit as hard as Dad to find the real killer."

Abby nodded. "I'd better get back to the rest of the guests." She gave Sheila a hug. "Thanks, Sheila, for being a good friend."

It was about an hour later that Abby stepped out onto the porch to get a breath of fresh air. She immediately spied Junior leaning against the corral railing. She walked over to him, noticing how the midday sun emphasized his years. For the first time since she could ever remember, he looked old and tired.

"I heard you're relieving yourself from Greg's case," she said in greeting.

He flashed her a tired smile. "If I'm to guess, you've been talking to Sheila. There isn't any barrier between what my daughter hears and what she says...it just kind of all flows in and out spontaneously."

Abby smiled at the apt characterization of Sheila. "She's a good friend."

He nodded. "And I have a feeling you're going to need some good friends now."

"That bad?" Abby's heart quickened with dread.

"Not good." Junior heaved a deep sigh. "We've got a dead man, witnesses to your threats, and a murder weapon that could only have come from your barn."

"Lots of people have access to the branding irons," Abby protested.

"That's true, but lots of people didn't have a motive for wanting Greg dead. Motive, Abby, that's what seems to be lacking with everyone but you. Hell, half the people on this ranch didn't even know Greg. He hadn't been in town long enough to make anyone mad enough to kill him."

"Don't underestimate Greg's charm. In a matter of minutes he could make a saint angry," Abby replied dryly.

"You don't have to tell me about Greg Foxwood's character. I was here when he left you, I remember how he broke your heart."

"But that was years ago and the punishment for breaking a woman's heart isn't death."

"But Greg did threaten to take Cody away from you, didn't he?" Junior eyed her sharply.

"Yes, but do you really think I'd telegraph my intentions by yelling them to a bunch of people in a diner, then go out and follow through on my threats?"

"It doesn't matter what I think, and most officials will tell you these kinds of crimes aren't always committed with forethought. I just know that's the motive that a prosecutor will use. He'll say you two argued

in the diner and you went to Greg's room to finish
the argument. Things got out of control and you
smashed him in the head.''

"But that's not what happened. Somebody else met
Greg in his motel room and somebody else hit him
with a poker from this ranch.''

"It doesn't help that you've got no alibi that can
be corroborated.''

"I've got the truth," Abby replied.

Junior looked at her sadly. "I'm not sure in this
case your truth is going to be enough.''

LUKE SAT on several bales of hay just outside the
barn, his attention captured by Abby and the sheriff
talking by the corral.

"My daddy's dead.''

He jumped at the sound of the boyish voice and
turned to see Abby's son standing near the end of the
hay bales. "I know." He looked back at Abby, noting
the way the sun played on the pale hue of her hair,
how her long dress hugged her tall slenderness. The
ruffled bodice and sleeves gave her an overall innocent appeal, but Luke wasn't fooled.

"Are you a daddy?''

Cody's voice interrupted Luke's thoughts and he
frowned at the boy. "No. I'm not a daddy.''

Apparently not put off by the frown as Luke had
hoped, the boy scrambled up next to him on the bale
of hay. He brought with him the scent of boyhood,
of sunshine and innocent mischief, of lemon fabric
softener and rich black dirt. "I feel bad 'cause I don't
feel bad...about my daddy, I mean. Everybody keeps

saying 'poor little boy' but I don't feel like a poor little boy. I'm sorry my daddy is dead, but I never even saw him ever once in my whole life.''

Luke's stomach clenched tightly at Cody's words. He knew well what it was like not to know his father. He understood the gnawing emptiness that would follow Cody into adulthood. He understood it because it lived in him.

''Are you a real cowboy or not?''

''I didn't know there was any other kind,'' Luke answered.

''Mom says there's two kinds. The real kind and the pretend kind.''

Despite his reluctance, Luke found himself curious. ''What's the difference?''

Cody clicked the heels of his boots together, like Dorothy wishing herself home from Oz. ''Mom says the pretend cowboys dress the part, walk the walk and talk the talk, but they don't live by the cowboy creed.''

''The cowboy creed?''

Cody nodded solemnly. ''You know, stuff like always tell the truth and don't hurt other people and love the land and your horse.'' He hesitated a moment, then added with a toothless grin, ''Oh, yeah, and love your mom.''

Luke looked away from the kid, not wanting to be sucked into the sweet innocence in his eyes. Cody's eyes held not only the childish ability to dream, but also the ability to believe in his dreams. His smile held an appeal that, if Luke allowed, would pierce through Luke's soul to any softness that might remain there, and Luke couldn't afford that. He couldn't afford to care about this tow-haired moppet, not with the way he felt about Abby.

Luke looked back toward the corral, only to realize that at some point Abby and the sheriff had apparently returned to the house.

He plucked out a piece of hay and chewed it thoughtfully, wishing he'd been privy to whatever conversation the two had shared. He glanced at the kid beside him, surprised to see that Cody had positioned himself exactly like Luke, right down to the piece of hay in his mouth.

Luke stood and threw the hay away, needing to distance himself from this boy with his sweet youthful scent and sunshine smile. At that moment Abby stepped out onto the porch. She scanned the area, her gaze stopping when it landed on Luke and her son.

She walked toward them in purposeful strides, the waning afternoon sun painting her in lush gold tones. Again Luke was struck with wonder at how such outer beauty could hide such a selfish, black heart.

"Cody, Bulldog is looking for you. I think he wanted to play some catch," she said as she approached the two.

Cody flashed a quicksilver smile to Luke as he scrambled down from the bales. "Bulldog is my best friend even though he's a grown-up."

Luke nodded. Bulldog was one of the ranch hands. Although as big and strong as a mountain, it hadn't taken Luke long to realize the man was slow.

"I hope he wasn't bothering you," Abby said after Cody had disappeared around the back of the house.

Luke shrugged, unsure how to answer the question. *Yes, he was bothering me because I don't want to like him or you.* Or, *No, he wasn't bothering me because I refuse to be affected by the innocence of a child.*

She sank onto the bale of hay and he noted the lines of stress that furrowed her brow. "This has all been difficult on him. He doesn't know how to react to everything that's happened."

"There's a big crowd here. Your ex-husband must have had a lot of friends."

Her eyes narrowed. "Greg didn't have friends. He only had marks...people he could suck money and favors from."

"Didn't your mother ever tell you it's rude to speak ill of the dead?"

"My mother's dead," she said stiffly, then sighed. "But you're right. Not only do I not want to talk ill of the dead, after today I don't want to talk about Greg at all."

Cold. How easily she was able to dismiss the man who'd been her husband, the father of her son. And how amazing that he could feel a lick of lust stir inside him as he gazed at her creamy complexion, the fullness of her lips, the azure blue of her eyes. Lust coupled with hate. An interesting combination.

"I'd better get back inside," she said as she stood. "The guests are starting to leave." She turned to leave but he stopped her by placing a hand on her arm.

Warm. Her skin was warm and soft beneath his touch. It surprised him. He hadn't expected her warmth. A swift arrow of desire shot through him. "If you get lonely, you know where to find me."

She pulled away from him, a blush once again darkening her cheeks. "I don't get lonely," she replied.

He watched as she walked back to the house, her hips softly swaying beneath her dress. Lust and hatred. Definitely an intriguing combination.

He crossed his boots and plucked another piece of hay to chew. He intended to follow through on both emotions. He could satisfy one while entertaining the other. A vision of Cody's face filled his head and he shoved it away. He couldn't let his resolve waver, couldn't allow any softness in his own hard heart. He intended to destroy Abby Connor and he couldn't allow anything to get in his way.

Abby ran, her breaths coming in harsh pants as she tried to get away from Greg. He bellowed rage from behind her and when she turned to look at him he was no longer Greg, but a skeleton.

Around her the landscape changed before her eyes, the trees coming to life, reaching out their limbs with evil intent, trying to capture her. The ground writhed beneath her and the grass became fingers grasping her feet, impeding her escape.

"Help me," she cried, but her words came out of her mouth in large bubbles, like comic strip thoughts, and shattered as they hit the ground.

Greg yelled once again and when she turned around to see him, he'd become a branding iron.

Luke held the branding iron. "Just have dinner with me and he'll go away," Luke said.

She watched in horror as Luke's features melted and he became Junior. "Just tell me the truth, Abby girl. Tell me how you killed him." Then the branding iron was in her hand and it was covered with blood.

Abby fell to the ground, too exhausted to run any farther. She squeezed her eyes closed, the brilliant sensory madness making her ill.

She awoke slowly, fighting her way up from the darkness of her dreams. Dreams. A wave of relief raced through her as she realized they'd just been horrid, disturbing, crazy dreams.

The relief lasted only a moment. Her cheek was pressed against cool earth and dewy grass tickled her nose. She opened her eyes, horror sweeping through her as she found herself lying in the middle of the front yard.

She sat up, confusion sweeping away the last of the horrific nightmare images. How had she gotten here? The last thing she remembered was drinking a cup of hot chocolate, then getting into bed.

She stood, slightly woozy and looked around, seeking some kind of answer for how she had come to be in the middle of the yard in the middle of the night.

Overhead the quarter moon spilled a faint light but offered no answers. Her nightgown was damp with dew, attesting to the fact she'd been outside for some time. Her lungs hurt, as if she'd been running for miles. Dear God, what had happened? How had she gotten here?

As she took a tentative step, a pain shot out from

the bottom of her foot. She limped toward the house, realizing she must have cut or bruised it somehow. She paused on the porch and raised her foot to see the bottom. Dried blood surrounded a jagged tear. How had she cut it? Closing her eyes, she drew a deep, steadying breath.

Why couldn't she remember? She sank onto a wicker chair and wrapped her arms around herself, staring out into the darkness of the night.

Had she sleepwalked? She couldn't ever remember doing anything like this before. If she'd been asleep, why hadn't she awakened when she cut her foot? Nausea rumbled in the pit of her stomach and she swallowed several times against it.

As the images she'd dreamed swept through her mind once again, she shivered and wrapped her arms around herself.

Had it been a dream...or something more insidious? She remembered the night of Greg's murder. She'd driven to Walker's pond and had sat staring at the calm, smooth surface of the water. Two hours later she'd come to, thinking she must have fallen asleep.

Was it possible she'd sleepwalked that night? That somehow while thinking she'd been sleeping she'd actually driven her car to Greg's rented room and killed him, then driven back to the pond and awakened with no memory of the act?

"No." The single word of denial escaped from her on a desperate whisper. No, she couldn't have killed Greg. She would have known if she had, she would remember.

But you don't remember how you got into the yard, a small voice niggled in her head. *You don't remember cutting your foot.*

She clapped her hands over her ears, as if by that act alone she could quiet the terrifying voice in her head. *I sleepwalked,* she told herself firmly. Tonight had been a single anomaly, a result of all the stress she'd been under. She'd had nothing to do with Greg's death.

To think otherwise was to flirt with madness.

Chapter Four

"Luke asked for a ride into town and we told him we were sure it would be fine," Colette said when Abby met her, Hank and the baby at the car the next afternoon. "Since you're driving us to the airport, I didn't think you'd mind him tagging along," she explained. "I know you have some shopping to do and at least he'll be some company on the ride back home."

Bad company, Abby thought, irritated that Luke had managed to manipulate his way into the ride. "Where is he?" she asked, looking at her watch. "We don't want you to be late for your flight."

"Relax, we have plenty of time. He just ran back to the bunkhouse for something." Colette linked arms with her husband and gave him a lingering, intimate smile that caused a stir of envy in Abby. Oh, to have somebody to love her, to hold her while she battled the craziness that had become her life.

As Hank and Colette talked softly of their travel plans and they all waited for Luke to return to the car, Abby found herself ruminating over her sleepwalking the night before.

By the time dawn had crept into her bedroom, she'd managed to convince herself it had been an isolated incident, brought on solely by the trauma of the past several days.

She knew with a certainty she couldn't be responsible for Greg's death. She didn't have that kind of anger, of hatred, inside her, didn't have the rage that would be required to commit murder.

Yes, Greg had frightened her with his talk of taking Cody, he'd angered her with his games of manipulation. Yes, she'd made crazy, rage-filled threats, but never had there been murder in her heart.

"Ah, here he comes," Colette said, pulling Abby from her thoughts.

Abby turned to see Luke approaching them, his loose-hipped walk again creating a flutter of unexpected heat in Abby's stomach. Beneath the rim of his hat, his eyes glittered with a wicked light, as if he knew she knew he'd manipulated Hank and Colette into letting him ride along.

"Abby." He tipped his hat in mock politeness.

She nodded curtly and got into the driver seat, further irritated when Hank and Colette got in the back with the baby, leaving Luke the passenger seat. When he got in, the interior of the car instantly seemed to shrink.

Abby had never met a man with so much physical presence, a man who affected her so deeply in a purely carnal way. Something about Luke Black made her ache with a need long suppressed and it irritated the hell out of her.

Luke swept his hat off his head and turned partway

in the seat to look at Hank, Colette and their baby girl. "So, I hear you two are off for a belated honeymoon," he said.

"That's right," Colette answered. "We did things a little backward. I had the baby first, then we got married and now the three of us are honeymooning together." Abby heard the love in her sister's voice. "It took this hardheaded man of mine a long time to decide what he wanted."

Hank's deep, husky laughter resounded. "Don't let her fool you. The minute I looked into her eyes, I was a doomed man. What about you, Luke? Got a special woman in your life?"

"I'm working on it."

Abby felt his gaze on her and tightened her grip on the steering wheel. The man was absolutely shameless.

"What about family?" Hank asked.

Luke's gaze left Abby and he stared out the window. "Nope. No family." His clipped words invited no further questions on that particular subject.

The ride to the airport took about thirty minutes. Thirty minutes of small talk between the others while Abby focused on ignoring Luke's presence. She dreaded the moment when Colette and Hank would get on the plane and she'd be left with Luke's company. But all too soon that moment came.

As she hugged and kissed Colette, Hank and the baby goodbye at the boarding gate, she was aware of Luke standing off to one side. Although his hat once again hid his eyes, his lips were curved upward in a slightly mocking smile.

"Where was it you needed to go in town?" she asked as they got back in the car.

"Wherever you're going is fine with me."

"Playing games, Mr. Black?" Abby asked with an arched brow.

He grinned, this time a full, heart-stopping smile. "I'm an advocate of using whatever works to get what I want."

"And just what exactly do you want?"

"You."

His answer caused Abby's mouth to dry and her throat to momentarily constrict. She coughed out a sharp laugh. "You're crazy. You don't even know me."

"I know what I like, and I like cool blondes with long, sexy legs."

Abby pulled to a stop in front of the feed store. She shut off the car's engine then turned to the man sitting next to her. "Luke, I suppose I should be flattered by your interest, but I'm not in the market for a summer fling with a drifter cowboy. I lived that particular fantasy once and it turned into a nightmare."

"What do you mean?"

Abby shook her head, not wanting to get into the heartache of Greg's desertion, the loss of dreams and happily-ever-after. "It really doesn't matter. Look, I've got a ranch that's teetering on the brink of financial ruin and I'm the number one suspect in a murder investigation. The last thing I need or want in my life right now is a relationship of any kind with any man."

He reached out and touched the pulse point pounding in the hollow of her throat. "Then why is your pulse racing?"

His touch was warm and his masculine scent surrounded her. For a moment Abby remained unmoving, her gaze locked with his, her heartbeat quickened to a frantic pace. "I...I need to go into the store." Her voice sounded faint, faraway.

"Then you'd better go," he replied, his fingers still touching the base of her throat, then moving up to softly stroke her cheek.

"I'm going."

It wasn't until he dropped his hand that the inertia that gripped Abby fell away. She scooted out of the car as if on fire, irritated with him for touching her, but more irritated with herself for her immediate and turbulent response to his touch.

As she headed for the store, she was aware of him getting out of the car and following her, that damnable little smile curving his lips. Drat the man anyway.

She didn't need this kind of complication in her life. She entered Wiley's Feed Store, immediately embraced by the scents of grains and leather goods. As she wandered up one aisle and down another, Luke Black consumed her thoughts.

No, she didn't need the complication of a man in her life, but how sweet it would be to be held in strong arms, to allow passion to override all her worries. How wonderful it would be to share both her fears and her dreams with a special man.

But not a man like Luke Black. Oh, no. If and when

she ever decided to gamble her heart again, she'd risk it to a banker or a lawyer, somebody who wouldn't heed the call of the wind and ride off when the vagabond spirit moved him.

She shook her head to clear thoughts of Luke away and instead focused on the things she needed to pick up for the ranch. She needed to buy a new gardening hoe. As she picked through the selection, Luke stood next to her, his very closeness distracting her.

"Here, let me," he said as she chose the hoe she wanted. He carried it and followed her as she picked out a few more supplies.

"That should do it," she said as they approached Walter Wiley, who stood behind the cash register like a wooden cigar store statue.

"Good afternoon, Walter," she greeted the tall, somber-faced man.

"Abby." He nodded curtly.

"Would you put this on my tab?"

He frowned. "Abby, I told you last time you were in that you needed to take care of your tab. I can't give you any more credit until you pay some of your balance."

"But I did." Abby frowned in confusion. "I wrote out a check a week or two ago." She distinctly remembered writing the check. "Didn't Rusty bring it in?"

Walter shook his head. "I didn't get a check and you don't get no more credit."

"Just ring up the purchases, we'll pay cash," Luke said. As he pulled a handful of bills from his pocket, Abby fought a wave of embarrassment.

"I'll repay you just as soon as we get back to the ranch," Abby said as she opened the car trunk and Luke stowed the purchases inside.

"Don't worry about it," he said as she slammed shut the trunk. "I kind of like the idea of you being beholden to me."

Abby ignored his statement. "What I'd like to know is what happened to the check I wrote to pay off that balance." She leaned against the car and rubbed her forehead. "I could have sworn I gave it to Rusty."

"Is it possible Rusty somehow managed to cash it?"

Abby shook her head. "He wouldn't do that. Rusty has been our foreman ever since I was a little girl. I trust him like I trust all the members of my family. I guess it's possible he stuck the check someplace and forgot to bring it in. I'll ask him about it when we get back."

"Where else do you need to go?"

"Grocery store. I promised Maria I'd pick up a few things for her, and I know there's no problem with our account there."

He grinned. "Too bad. I thought perhaps I could deepen your debt to me."

"Trust me, you'll get your money back. I go out of my way to live my life not indebted to anyone."

Dusk was falling by the time they finished getting groceries and started the drive home. "Why don't we stop at the diner and get something to eat before going back to the ranch?" Luke suggested.

Abby frowned. She hadn't been back to the diner

since the night of Greg's murder. Still, it was getting late, Luke would have missed supper for the ranch hands and Abby was in no mood to go home and rustle up something to eat. On the other hand, she hated facing the whispers and speculation that seemed to have become a part of her life since Greg's death.

"You already braved the worst of the whispers in the grocery store," Luke said, as if reading her mind.

"So you noticed." Abby sighed. "I don't understand it, these people have known me all my life. They know the kind of person I am. They've been my friends and acquaintances for years, but suddenly they're looking at me like they've never seen me before."

"Murder frightens people."

"If I was going to kill Greg, I certainly wouldn't have telegraphed my intentions by screaming threats in front of witnesses before accomplishing the act." Abby swung into the diner parking lot, having made up her mind to grab a bite to eat before venturing the rest of the way home. She'd be damned if she'd forgo the pleasure of a meal out because her neighbors suddenly found her fascinating.

"Some people will believe your passion got the better of you."

Abby laughed dryly and shut off the car engine. "I've never experienced the kind of passion that would make me do anything crazy." She opened her car door and got out.

Together they entered the diner and found a booth near the back. Abby was grateful the place was less crowded than usual. The dinner crowd had probably already come and gone, and the late evening coffee drinkers and pie eaters had yet to arrive.

"I'm ravenous," Luke said, but he made no move to pick up the menu, and his gaze made her think he wasn't talking about food.

She shoved a menu at him, refusing to be drawn into a game of innuendos and double entendres. She had far too much on her mind to indulge herself in a flirtation she didn't intend to follow through on.

"Hi, hon." Sheila waved from the counter. "I'll be with you two in a minute."

Abby nodded.

"She a close friend?" Luke asked as he took off his hat and placed it on the seat next to him. "I remember seeing her at the ranch after the funeral."

"Yes, we're good friends. Although actually, I'm closer to her father, the sheriff."

"How'd that happen? I mean, the sheriff isn't exactly in your peer group." He set the menu aside and looked at her curiously.

"Junior and my father were best friends. Not a day went by while I was growing up that they weren't hunting or fishing, or just sitting at our kitchen table drinking coffee together."

Abby paused and laced her hands together on top of the table. "I was eighteen when I got pregnant and Greg and I got married. Two months before that my parents had died in a car accident. Greg left when Cody was eight weeks old."

She paused again, this time to swallow against the bittersweet taste of painful memories. "God, that was a summer of such grief. Junior became the rock I clung to in order to survive.''

"Why did your husband leave you?"

Abby sighed. "I don't know. He didn't want to be a husband. He didn't want to be a father. He was angry because I wouldn't put the ranch in his name. He wanted me to sell the ranch, but I couldn't do that. It had been left to me in trust. It was not only Colette and Belinda's heritage, it was Cody's.''

She waved her hands dismissively. "I don't want to talk about this anymore. None of it matters now.''

"The past is never completely gone. It has a way of jumping up and biting you when you least expect it.''

Abby looked at him curiously. "What about you, Luke? Where are you from? What's in your past?"

She got no answers for at that moment Sheila appeared at their booth to take their orders.

IT WASN'T UNTIL their food had been served that Abby once again broached the subject. "You never answered me. Where are you from?"

"Back East."

"Could you be more vague?" she asked dryly.

He considered her question thoughtfully. Best if he stuck as near to the truth as possible, he decided. "Chicago. My last address was just outside Chicago.''

"Were you working on a ranch?"

"No, mostly warehouse work." A lie, but a fairly safe one. He couldn't tell her the truth, not until he got the information he needed. At the moment the need for revenge was secondary to the need for answers.

He thought of the stack of letters back in his bunkhouse, letters chronicling Abby Connor's selfishness, her heartlessness, letters that painted her as the kind of woman who could kill anyone who got in her way.

He needed to find out the truth, and the only way he knew to get to it was to get close to Abby, court her, force her to be vulnerable to him.

"What brought you to Cheyenne? To my ranch?"

Luke shrugged. "Fate. Chance. I left Chicago and drifted for a while, picking up work here and there. I made my way into Cheyenne and somebody mentioned you might need some hands at your ranch."

"And you mentioned on the way to the airport that you have no family?"

A lump grew in Luke's throat. He swallowed against it and tried to keep his voice as even as possible. "No family," he replied. He knew what the lump was…unacknowledged grief. Someday, someway, he'd have to face the grief in his life, but not now, not yet.

He watched Abby as she ate. She didn't pick at her food, or take dainty little bites. She ate with gusto, as if enjoying the act of appeasing hunger.

He had a feeling there was a wide river of passion in her, despite her protests to the contrary. He took a sip of his coffee, his gaze lingering on her thoughtfully.

He suspected she was guilty of killing Greg, and for that act alone she deserved nothing but his rancor, his revenge. However, there was something soft and vulnerable about her, as well. And it was that quality that would make his plans more difficult to stomach, harder to accomplish.

Still, he'd made a vow years ago, a vow he'd not lived up to. Redemption for him came in destroying her. But not until he was sure, and for that certainty he needed facts.

"The police haven't come up with any other leads on your ex-husband's murder?" he asked.

She shook her head, inner shadows deepening the blue of her eyes. "I don't think they're looking very hard for leads." She set her fork down as if his question had chased away her appetite. "I think the authorities have decided they already know who killed him and aren't looking hard for other suspects."

"Then why haven't you been arrested?"

She shrugged and stared down at the food remaining on her plate. "I don't know. I suppose a lack of evidence. What frightens me is that I think it's just a matter of time and I will be arrested." When she raised her gaze to his again, her eyes were haunted with fear.

Luke fought the impulse to reach across the table and take her hands in his, assure her it would all be okay. The last thing he wanted to feel for her was compassion. That particular emotion had no place in the scheme of things.

"I've got something for that boy of yours," Sheila said as she approached their table. She placed a foam box in front of Abby. "I know how Cody loves our chocolate pie, so you take this piece home for him."

"Thanks, Sheila. But he won't be able to eat it until

tomorrow. He's spending the night with Billy Wallace," Abby explained.

"How about some dessert for the two of you?" Sheila asked.

"None for me," Luke replied. Abby demurred, as well, and Luke asked for their check.

By the time they got back in the car and were headed for the ranch, night had fallen around them. Dark clouds skittered across the sky and hid the moon from view.

"Looks like rain," Luke observed.

"We could definitely use some." Abby pulled up in front of the house and parked the car. "Why don't you come on in and I'll get you a check for the things you bought in the feed store."

"Okay." He followed her inside the dark, quiet house. As she flipped on lights, he looked around with interest. The living room was large, with a lived-in look that immediately forecasted comfort.

He followed her down a hallway to a small office. As she rummaged in the drawer, Luke looked at the pictures that decorated the walls. Photographs of the Connor girls were everywhere, pictures chronicling their growing-up years. Abby was easy to pick out of each photo. Taller than her sisters, her arms were always around them protectively.

"You're very close to your sisters."

She looked up from the checkbook. "Yes. We've always had a special relationship. Growing up on a ranch with no other kids around formed an especially close bond." She focused back on her task of writing a check.

Envy raced through Luke. Familial ties were something he'd never felt, never experienced. Regret surged through him and with it an edge of anger...anger directed at Abby.

She straightened and tore the check out, then approached him. "Here you are. My debt to you paid in full."

He took the check from her and moved closer, consciously invading her space. A blush colored her cheeks and she swept past him and out of the room.

He followed, watching her hips sway softly in the jeans that molded to her like lover's hands. He knew she was conscious of his gaze, knew it by the way her back stiffened as she moved on wooden footsteps across the living room and to the front door.

She stepped out onto the front porch with him. The wind had picked up, portending a storm. It tousled her hair and carried her scent to him. In the nearby corral the horses kicked and neighed, as if they sensed the coming storm.

Lightning rent the sky in the distance, followed a moment later by a rumble of thunder. "You were right about the rain. Looks like we're in for a storm," she said.

"Definitely," he agreed, and stepped closer to her. "I can feel it in my blood...the wildness." He took another step toward her, now so close he could feel the heat from her. "Can't you feel it?"

Another flash of lightning illuminated her features for just a moment. Starkly lit, her gaze radiated a touch of desire, her lips parted in subconscious invitation.

"You didn't pay your debt to me in full," he said softly, his hands going to her shoulders.

"I didn't?" Whisper-soft, her voice was nearly lost to another roll of thunder.

He could tell she wanted him to kiss her, and he wanted the same thing. After all, it was the next step in his plan to get close to her, get her to trust him.

He hadn't lied to her about the storm...as he looked at her, smelled her sweet scent, felt her body heat reaching out to him, a wildness pounded in his veins. "With any debt, there's always interest to be paid."

Before she could reply, he dipped his head and captured her mouth with his. Initially, she held herself rigid, as if refusing to be moved by the kiss. He slid his hands down her back and pulled her intimately against him, at the same time deepening the kiss invasively.

She surrendered, the unyielding stiffness of her body giving way as she melted against him. The honeyed sweetness of her mouth, coupled with the pliant closeness of her body against his, caused his senses to roar and the initial, calculating reason why he'd wanted to kiss her to fade.

As she wound her arms around his neck, he felt as if he'd swallowed the storm. Lightning flashed in the pit of his stomach and thunder resounded in his rapid heartbeat.

He hadn't expected it. He hadn't expected the sweet desire that kissing her evoked. He hadn't anticipated the mind-numbing sensations that flooded through him.

A splash of raindrops caused her to gasp and pull away from him. "You shouldn't have done that," she said, the words coming out on a breathless gasp.

"I wasn't doing it alone," he said wryly.

She moved away from him. "Okay, we shouldn't have done that."

"Why not? I enjoyed it and you did, too."

"Yes, but I told you I have rules about getting involved with my workers."

He reached out and touched her mouth with his forefinger. "Rules are made to be broken. Sweet dreams, Abby." He didn't wait for a reply but instead turned and walked off the porch and toward the bunkhouse.

Abby watched him go, her lips still burning from his touch. She ducked inside the house, afraid the raindrops would sizzle as they hit her.

She locked the front door, then leaned heavily against it, waiting for her heartbeat to slow, her breathing to return to normal.

Oh, she'd forgotten. She'd forgotten how wonderful it felt to be in strong arms, how it felt to be pressed tightly against a male body. She'd forgotten how a mere kiss could send her senses reeling and stir desire to fever pitch. But it wasn't just any kiss. It had been Luke's kiss that had so stirred her.

She roused herself from the door and shut off the living room lights. As she walked down the hallway toward her bedroom, thunder once again boomed overhead.

Stepping into her room, she turned on the light as rain pelted her window. The rain was welcome. So far it had been a hot, dry summer and the cattle were having to scrounge to find grass. A good rain would help.

She pulled the curtains closed, her thoughts jumping back to Luke. As much as she hated to admit it, there was a part of her that reveled in his interest in her. It had been a long time since a man had looked at her with desire-filled eyes. Something about Luke filled her not only with a sweet passion, but also with a feeling of inexplicable dread.

She'd promised herself a long time ago that she'd never again risk her heart to love. But loneliness makes a cold bedfellow, she thought as she changed into her nightgown.

Luke was not a good bet on which to wager her heart. No family. No ties. When the harsh Wyoming winter swept the area, he'd probably leave.

The phone rang and she jumped in surprise at the unexpected sound. Diving across the bed she grabbed the receiver, hoping the noise hadn't awakened Belinda.

"Hello?" she answered. There was a moment of silence.

"It's me. Greg."

Abby gasped in horror and dropped the phone. Lightning blinded her momentarily and thunder crashed overhead. For a moment Abby felt as if the world as she knew it had tilted, plunging her into an abyss of madness. It had been Greg's voice. Dear God, how had her ex-husband managed to call her from beyond the grave?

Chapter Five

Abby stared at the phone, waiting...dreading the fact that it might ring again. She was unable to grasp how... How was it possible it had been Greg's voice on the line? And yet she knew his voice, knew it as well as she knew her own.

Minutes ticked by, agonizing minutes. But the phone remained mute. Had she imagined the whole thing? Lightning slashed the sky outside her window, followed by a rumble of thunder that sounded like low, demented laughter.

She wrapped her arms around herself, fighting off a shiver of fear. Once again she wondered if the stress of the past several days was playing with her sanity. Had the phone rung, or had it only been a figment of her imagination?

Pulling herself up off the bed, she tried to still the frantic throb of her heart. Calm. She needed to be calm. She couldn't think with terror filling her mind. She left her room and went down the hallway to Belinda's. Not bothering to knock on the door, she opened it and made her way across the dark room to the bed.

"Belinda?"

The lump beneath the covers didn't move.

"Belinda?" Abby reached out and gently shook the sleeping woman.

"Wha..." Belinda reluctantly stirred. Abby reached over and turned on the lamp beside the bed. Belinda groaned and flung an arm across her face to shield her eyes. "Abby, what's wrong?"

"Did you hear the phone ring a few minutes ago?"

Belinda sat up, squinting against the glare of the light. "I was sleeping, I didn't hear anything. Why?"

"I got a phone call a few minutes ago." Abby hesitated, then drew a deep breath. "It was Greg."

Belinda stared at her. "Abby, that's impossible. Greg is dead."

"I know...I know, but it was his voice."

"What did he say?"

"He just said, 'It's me. Greg.' Then I hung up." Abby stared at her sister, wanting Belinda to make sense from the madness, needing Belinda to come up with a reasonable explanation.

"Abby, honey. It was probably just a prank, kids causing mischief."

Abby frowned, wanting to believe, but no kid could have managed to duplicate Greg's voice. And it had been Greg's voice. "It didn't sound like any kid. It sounded like Greg."

Belinda placed a hand on Abby's shoulder. "Abby, you've had a rough week. Your mind probably isn't as clear as it normally is. Greg is dead and dead men don't make phone calls."

"Of course, you're right." Abby stood, sorry she'd

awakened Belinda. Kids. It had to have been kids and because Abby was stressed, she'd imagined it sounded exactly like Greg. "I'm sorry I bothered you. Go back to sleep." She turned off the light and realized her sister was already once again asleep.

Abby wasn't so lucky. Sleep didn't come easy to her. She sat in her room, afraid to turn off the lights, afraid Greg might call again, afraid she was losing her mind.

The storm passed with the darkness of the night, and the last of the rain clouds skittered away as the sun peeked over the horizon.

By the time dawn arrived, Abby had managed to convince herself Belinda had been right. The phone call had been a prank. Besides, she had other things to worry about, like another day of trying to keep the ranch running smoothly.

As she showered, she remembered Luke and the passion-filled kiss that had rocked her to the core, stirred her senses as they hadn't been stirred in years.

Was he truly interested in pursuing a real relationship with her, or was he merely passing time, indulging in summer passion before moving on with his life?

Every man came with a past, but Luke seemed reluctant to talk about his. She knew almost nothing about him, except that his gaze held a heat that warmed her, and his lips had tasted like wild desire.

She'd sworn to herself she'd never get involved with another cowboy, never trust her heart to the whims of a drifter. But rules are meant to be broken.

Luke's words came back to her, whispering a sweet seduction in her ear.

She turned the water to a blast of cold, cooling any heat the memory of Luke's kiss had evoked. One day at a time. She'd learned to survive by living that adage.

Once dressed, she decided to find Rusty and ask him about the Wiley's Feed Store bill. Before heading out to Rusty's quarters, she stopped in the office to look over the checkbook. As she thumbed through the stubs, she realized several checks were missing and unrecorded.

She frowned, irritated with herself. She'd been lax lately, not thinking clearly since she'd heard Greg was back in town. She'd have to be more careful about recording payments. Hopefully when she got her next bank statement, she'd be able to straighten things out.

Outside the air smelled sweet and fresh and the sun beat warmly on her back as she walked to the separate building where Rusty lived. As foreman, unlike the rest of the hands, Rusty didn't reside in the bunkhouse, but rather had his own living space in what had once been the old smokehouse.

Although small, with a bathroom and a kitchenette that had been added over the years, the smokehouse was apparently all the old man needed, for he'd never complained.

Abby knocked on the door, hoping she wasn't so early he was still in bed. He answered immediately. "Miss Abby." She rarely came here and surprise was evident on his face. "Uh...come in. I was just getting ready to have a cup of coffee before heading to work."

Abby stepped inside the small room, curious to see the place Rusty called home. A single bed served double duty as sleeping space at night and makeshift sofa during the day. A portable television sat on an end table, an easy chair filled out the remaining space in the room.

"Would you like a cup of coffee?" Rusty asked as he went to the area that contained an apartment-size stove and refrigerator.

For a man who'd lived in this place for fifteen years, Rusty had made no permanent personal mark. No pictures, no knickknacks or favorite items appeared anywhere in sight. Funny, she thought, that Rusty had spent so many years on the ranch working for the Connors, and Abby knew no more about him than she did any of the workers who drifted in and out with the seasons.

"Miss Abby?" Rusty held up a coffee cup.

"Oh, no, thanks," she said, pulling her thoughts back to the matter at hand. "Rusty, I went into Wiley's Feed Store yesterday and he told me we hadn't paid our bill. Didn't I give you a check to take care of that a couple of weeks ago?"

Rusty frowned, his gray eyebrows pulling together to form a single line across his brow. "I don't remember you giving me a check for Wiley's."

"Are you sure? It's so clear in my mind. We were standing in the office and I handed you the check and told you to pay off our account."

Rusty shook his head thoughtfully. "No, I don't

remember that at all.'' His face lit up. ''Oh, maybe you're thinking about when you gave me the check for the fencing supplies we bought a couple weeks ago.''

Abby sighed and rubbed the center of her forehead. She would swear she'd given that check to Rusty. The scene was so clear, so vivid in her mind. But she was also aware that her mind hadn't exactly been trustworthy of late. ''Perhaps,'' she finally said. After all, what possible reason could Rusty have to lie about it? A phone rang. ''I'll just get out of here and let you answer that.''

Rusty shrugged. ''The answering machine will get it.''

''No, that's all right. Go on, and I'll get out of your hair.''

As she walked back to the house, she once again replayed the scene in her head. She distinctly remembered handing Rusty a check and telling him to pay the Wiley bill, but she also remembered a phone call from a dead man.

Stifling a yawn with the back of her hand, she decided she definitely needed a jolt of caffeine if she intended to make it through the day without a nap.

''Morning, Abby.''

She jumped at the familiar deep male voice coming from the shadows by the barn. Luke stepped into the dawn light, an intimate smile playing on his lips.

''Good morning.'' She didn't slow her pace, didn't feel up to bantering with him after her sleepless night. Her mind was already too confused. At the moment she didn't need or want the additional confusion Luke Black brought her.

"Sleep well?" he asked, falling into step beside her.

"Not particularly." She lengthened her stride, but his long legs easily paced her.

"Let me guess. You tossed and turned all night, wishing our kissing hadn't stopped."

Abby halted and faced him. "It might surprise you, Luke, but I have other things on my mind besides your kisses."

The smile fell from his lips as his gaze searched her face. "What's wrong, Abby?"

For just a moment Abby wanted to lean into him, allow him to pull her into his arms so she could absorb some strength. She wanted to tell him she'd sleepwalked and wound up in the yard, that last night she'd heard Greg's voice on the telephone, that she remembered things that hadn't happened and didn't remember things that might have happened.

"I just have a lot on my mind this morning," she finally answered.

"It's more than that," he countered. He reached out and touched her cheek. "I can see it in your eyes."

She batted his hand away, disturbed by the heat that immediately swirled through her at his touch. "I'm just tired," she said. "Nothing more." She whirled around to leave. "Tell Rusty to have one of the men saddle up Blackheart. I'll be out later to take a ride."

Luke watched her disappear through the back door

of the house. Something was bothering her. Guilt? Fear? Various emotions had radiated from her eyes, shown in the stress lines of her face. Murder would do that to a person. Sooner or later she'd break completely, unable to handle the heaviness of her guilt. He intended to be with her when it happened. And he intended to be the one to turn her over to the authorities when it happened.

"I saw you last night."

Luke jumped and swore at the voice coming from behind him. He turned to see Bulldog glaring at him. "You saw me what last night?"

Bulldog took a step closer to Luke, bringing with him the sweet scent of the peppermints the man ate all the time. "I saw you kissing Miss Abby."

"That's right, I did kiss Miss Abby last night."

"You ain't gonna hurt her, are you?"

"By kissing her? Nah."

Bulldog frowned, frustration evident on his blunt features. "I know kissing doesn't hurt, but you know what I mean. I don't want you messing around with Miss Abby and making her cry."

"Did Greg make her cry?"

Bulldog's eyes narrowed. "That man was a devil. He broke Miss Abby's heart in a million different ways." Bulldog shoved a hand into his pocket and withdrew a piece of candy. "I may not be too smart, but I'm smart enough to know a devil when I see one, and Greg was a devil." He popped the candy into his mouth. "And I'm glad he's dead." He started to walk away, then turned to face Luke once again. "I might not be too smart, but I'm smart enough to hunt you down and make you pay if you hurt Miss Abby." This time when he turned to walk away, he didn't look back.

Luke watched him go. As big as a mountain, Bulldog was a curious mix of man and boy. Luke knew Bulldog was most comfortable when in Cody's company, playing boyhood games that required minimal intelligence and maximum imagination and energy.

Bulldog's loyalty to the Connor sisters was undeniable. Was it intense enough for him to kill a man he considered the very devil himself?

For the first time Luke entertained the thought that perhaps Abby wasn't guilty of the murder. Still, even if she didn't actually kill Greg, she had much to do with his final fall. He didn't intend to let up on her, but he did intend to keep an eye on Bulldog. If the man had killed Greg, Luke didn't think he had the social skills to cover his tracks, to consistently lie. Eventually he would trip up.

Luke walked over and leaned against the side of the barn. It was just a matter of time and he'd know who'd committed the murder. And Luke had all the time in the world to wait for the guilty to be brought to justice.

An hour later as Luke pounded nails to strengthen the corral railing, he saw Abby come out of the house and head in his direction. Blackheart danced in the corral, already saddled and awaiting a run.

Luke paused in his work and shoved his hat to the back of his head, watching her approach. Whether guilty or innocent, something about Abby Connor definitely stirred desire in him. Although he wanted to

believe her to be a coldhearted witch, what he saw
was a strong woman with too much vulnerability in
her eyes. Which was the real Abby Connor?

"He looks eager for a run," Luke said, gesturing
to the prancing black horse.

"And I'm hoping a good run will blow the cob-
webs out of my head. Two cups of coffee didn't do
the trick," she said as she unlatched the gate and
entered the corral.

Blackheart immediately walked over to her and
nuzzled her shirt pocket. "Ah, you're a spoiled one,"
she said softly as she pulled a lump of sugar from her
pocket and offered it to the horse.

"If you'd talk so sweet to me, I'd let you ride on
my back," Luke observed with a wry grin.

She turned around and looked at him, a hint of
amusement in her gaze. "If I were going to ride on
your back, I think I'd need spurs and a whip to maintain control."

"I suppose that could be intriguing, if that's your
taste."

"You're incorrigible," Abby replied, a blush stain-
ing her cheeks.

"Something about you makes me that way, and I
think something about me makes you feel the same."

"I think it sounds like you suffer from an abun-
dance of ego. The best cure I know for that is good
hard labor." She eyed the hammer and nails point-
edly.

Luke laughed and picked up his hammer, although
his gaze remained on her. He watched as she petted

the horse and whispered in his ear, then moved to the side to mount.

With one smooth movement, she swung her leg over the horse's back and settled in the saddle. At the same moment her bottom hit the saddle, Blackheart's eyes rolled back in his head and with a scream he reared up on his hind legs. As his front hooves hit the dirt, his back legs kicked out, unseating Abby and flinging her like a rag doll into the air. She curled up in a protective ball and landed on her back with a dull thud that stirred dust around her.

"Abby!" Luke tossed the hammer aside and raced to where she'd been thrown.

As he reached her, she sat up, gasping for breath. "I'm...I'm all right. I'll be okay...but please, get Blackheart...something's wrong with him."

Despite the fact that Blackheart had managed to dislodge Abby from his back, the horse still bucked and kicked, eyes rolling wildly as he emitted high-pitched neighs of distress.

Luke struggled to contain the animal in the corner of the corral, at the same time trying to grab the reins to gain control. He finally managed to get hold of the reins, only to have Abby take them from him.

"It's okay, baby. It's all right, sweetheart." She spoke in a low, soothing voice as she rubbed the horse's nose. "See if you can get the saddle off him."

The horse gentled as Abby continued to soothe and stroke and Luke managed to unfasten the girth and slide the saddle from his back. When he pulled off the blanket, he instantly saw what had caused Black-heart's distress. He pulled the tack nail from the horse's hide, the end of the nail bloody from where it had punctured Blackheart's skin.

"What the hell?" He held up the offensive nail to Abby.

She paled and moved to check the wound on Blackheart's back. "I want to get some salve on this, then I want to know who saddled up Blackheart this morning." As she led Blackheart into the barn and toward his stall, Luke followed.

"Abby, are you sure you're all right? You took quite a fall."

She paused at a cabinet and pulled out a jar of medicine. "I'm fine. I'll probably be sore tomorrow, but for now I'm fine." She got Blackheart settled in his stall, then put the salve on the wound, her features darkening as she worked.

Luke held the nail in his hand, wondering how in the hell it had gotten beneath her saddle blanket. Apparently the nail hadn't pierced Blackheart's hide until she'd sat down. It had either been carefully positioned, or it was a freak accident that could have had deadly consequences. Had Abby been a less experienced rider, her neck could have been broken in the fall.

Surely it had been a freak accident. Nothing else made sense. Besides himself, who else would have a motive to harm Abby? And even his own desire didn't include physical harm to her.

He watched as she finished up with the horse, then he followed her back outside. Anger wafted from her. Her eyes snapped and her footsteps were heavy with it. "Rusty." She yelled to the old man who, with several other hands, was loading a wagon with fence material. He left the men and approached where Abby and Luke stood.

"Rusty, who saddled Blackheart this morning?" she asked, her words clipped with emotion.

"I had Billy Sims do it. Why, there a problem?"

"Tell Billy I want to talk to him." Abby's voice radiated a strength without vulnerability, an anger not tainted with any other emotion.

It took Rusty only a minute to walk back to the wagon and instruct Billy that Abby wanted to speak with him. Billy Sims approached them with a sullen sneer on his face. When he got closer, Luke was able to smell the scent of soured alcohol that clung to him. His eyes were bloodshot. He looked like a man coming off a two-week drunk.

"Billy, you saddled Blackheart this morning?" Abby asked.

"Yeah, why?" Billy's red eyes radiated a dullness.

"You're fired."

Both Luke and Billy looked at her in surprise. "For what?" Billy asked, all dullness gone as anger tightened his features.

Abby gestured for Luke to give her the nail. She held it up for Billy to see. "This was in Blackheart's back, stuck beneath the saddle and blanket. Not only could I have been killed when I climbed on Blackheart's back, but the horse is hurt where the nail punctured him."

"I didn't put no nail under the saddle," Billy protested.

"It doesn't matter whether you put it there or not.

You should have seen it, you should have been more careful," Abby retorted.

"Ah, Miss Abby, don't fire me. You know I got no place else to go."

"Billy, I warned you last time that there would be no more second chances. I can't have a man who's drinking working here."

Luke noticed no charity in her eyes, rather they were a cold, arctic blue.

Billy's eyes filled with tears and his lips trembled. "Please, Miss Abby. Just give me one more chance. I swear I didn't see that nail. I didn't know it was there."

"I'm sorry, Billy, but I've already given you too many chances and you keep proving me wrong. Pack your things and come by the office before you leave. I'll pay you what you're owed."

As Abby turned to walk away, Luke realized he'd just seen the cold, heartless woman he'd heard about before arriving at the ranch. He'd just seen a woman who might very well be capable of murder.

Chapter Six

Abby walked around to the porch and leaned heavily against the railing. She hated having to fire people. She felt sick inside as she remembered the desperate look on Billy's face. But he'd left her no choice. She'd warned him time and again to stop his drinking. She'd overlooked too many careless mistakes and could do it no longer.

"You were pretty rough on him." Luke joined her on the porch.

She nodded. "And now you know how I got my reputation. Somebody has to be willing to do the difficult jobs." She sank onto the wicker chair. "I can't let Billy stay on any longer. He's made too many mistakes and sooner or later his mistakes will be costly. I can't depend on a man who drinks all night then tries to work hung over."

"Then it sounds like you did the right thing."

"If I were a man, it would be the right thing to do. Because I'm a woman, most of the workers will say it was a bitchy thing to do." She knew well how the ranch hands talked about her behind her back.

Luke smiled. "I have a feeling you can deal with the workers' opinions."

She shrugged. "I don't have a choice. I've got to make my decisions based on what's best for the ranch. Things are difficult enough around here without having to deal with a drunken ranch hand."

"I haven't seen your sister around this morning," Luke observed.

"She went into town to spend the day and tonight with a girlfriend." Abby knew with Colette married, and Abby so busy with the ranch and Cody, Belinda had been feeling rather displaced lately. She'd encouraged her to accept her friend's offer to spend a day and a night away from the ranch.

"Bulldog had a little talk with me this morning. He gave me a not-so-friendly warning."

Abby looked at him in surprise. "Bulldog? What on earth would Bulldog have to warn you about?"

"You." Luke leaned against the railing and shoved his hat back so his eyes were fully visible to her. "It seems Bulldog saw me kissing you last night. He warned me that if I hurt you he'd hunt me down and do me bodily harm."

Warmth swept up Abby's neck and burned her cheeks. "Bulldog can be a little overprotective."

"Overprotective enough to kill Greg?"

"Absolutely not," Abby replied without hesitation. "Bulldog doesn't have the capacity to harm anyone. He's got a gentle spirit and a loving heart."

"He didn't sound so loving when he spoke to me this morning," Luke replied.

"He loves us. My father took Bulldog in when he

was eighteen and his own family threw him out. Bulldog considers us his family, but even as much as he loves us, he's just not capable of violence.''

"Every man is capable of violence if pushed hard enough." His gaze was darkly intent as he stared at her. "I'll warrant most women are the same. Push hard enough, corner anyone, and their instincts are to fight back."

"Do you think I killed Greg?" Abby's breath pressed hard against her ribs as she awaited his answer. For some reason, it was important to her that he believe in her innocence.

"To be perfectly honest, I'm not sure what to think."

Abby nodded, slightly disappointed, but not surprised. After all, they had known each other less than a week. He'd hardly had enough time to assess her sum and total character. She drew in a breath and frowned as her gaze caught the rise of dust in the distance, portending a car approaching.

As the vehicle came into view, she realized it was not one car, but two. Two patrol cars with lights flashing official business, and they were headed for the ranch. "Oh, no, now what?"

Both Abby and Luke watched in silence as the cars pulled up in front of the house and Deputy Helstrom got out of the first car. Abby stood and took a step closer to Luke, as if he might offer some measure of protection from whatever was about to happen.

"Abby. I've got a search warrant here," Richard Helstrom said.

"A search warrant? For what?"

As an answer, Richard handed her a sheath of papers, then he and several other officers entered the house. "Wait..." Abby followed after them, her heart pounding violently.

"If you'll just point us to your bedroom, there's no reason to bother your sisters' things right now," Richard said.

Abby gestured toward her bedroom, feeling as if she'd been plunged headfirst into another nightmare. As the officers invaded her room, she leaned against the doorjamb. Luke came up behind her and placed a hand on her shoulder. As two officers began pulling clothes from her drawers, and Richard started removing items from her closet, she leaned back against Luke and closed her eyes, wishing herself far away.

Luke squeezed her shoulder, as if attempting to give her strength. Somehow it helped. She opened her eyes and stifled a groan as one of the officers dumped her underwear drawer on the bed. She suddenly wished they were multicolored silk and lace instead of serviceable white cotton.

She moved away from the door, away from Luke. "If you'll tell me what you're looking for, perhaps I can get it for you."

"I think I just found it," Richard said as he pulled one of her blouses from the closet. "Is this what you were wearing the night of Greg's death?"

"Yes...that blouse and a pair of jeans." Abby wondered how he knew that's what she'd worn. Had somebody described her outfit from that night in the diner? Did they expect to find something incriminating on the blouse?

She watched, her heart thudding painfully as Richard placed the blouse in a brown paper bag. He folded the top of the bag, then pulled another piece of paper from his breast pocket. "Abby Connor, I have a warrant here for your arrest for the murder of Greg Foxwood."

"No," Abby gasped. "No, please. This is all a mistake, a horrible mistake." Tears burned in her eyes and she turned to look at Luke, wanting him to do something, stop this madness before it advanced any further. His eyes held uncertain bewilderment and she knew there was nothing he could do for her.

She backed away, unbelieving as Richard read her the Miranda rights. She wanted to run, hide...escape from the tall deputy and his minions. This couldn't be happening. How could anyone really think she was guilty of Greg's death?

"Abby, don't make this any more difficult than it has to be," Richard said as he removed a set of handcuffs from his belt.

"But this is wrong. I didn't kill Greg. I swear, I had nothing to do with his death," Abby cried as Richard moved behind her to place her in the handcuffs.

"Is that really necessary?" Luke asked, his voice tense.

"Standard procedure," Richard answered.

The click of the handcuffs resounded in Abby's head at the same time the circles of steel bit into her flesh. She felt nauseous, faint, unable to believe this was happening. She fought against a rising panic.

Cody. Dear God, what would happen to Cody if she went to prison?

As Richard and the other officers led her out of the house, she turned frantically to Luke. "Maria went to stay with her sister who's been sick and I don't know when she'll be back. Please, you've got to take care of Cody for me. He'll be scared when he gets home and I'm not here. Promise me you'll take care of him until I get out or Belinda or Maria gets home."

Luke nodded. "I promise. You want me to call your sister and brother-in-law in Las Vegas?"

"No, there's no point. There's nothing they can do."

"Abby, you have a lawyer?" Luke asked.

"Yes, our family lawyer, although I don't know how good he is in criminal cases." She took a deep breath. "I'm sure he'll have me out of jail before nightfall." The optimism rang in her voice for only a moment, then despair once again flooded through her.

Tears flowed unchecked from her eyes as they walked outside and toward the waiting patrol cars. "The most important thing is for you to be here for Cody," she told Luke. "I don't want him to be afraid."

There were a million more things she wanted to say. She wanted to scream that she was innocent, cry that she was afraid. But she refused to give the ranch workers who'd gathered around, and the officers, the pleasure of seeing her break. Instead she swallowed her tears and straightened her shoulders. She'd be damned if she'd let any of them see her weak and afraid.

Richard opened the back door of his patrol car and Abby slid in, the handcuffs a painful distraction that lent a bite of reality to the surreal feel of the scene.

Within minutes the car pulled away. As the ranch fell behind, Abby's momentary burst of strength ebbed and fear once again swept through her. She'd never been in any legal or criminal trouble before. She feared not only the possibility of years behind bars, but the very process that might put her there.

What had Richard found on her blouse that had prompted him to arrest her? How was it possible for her to have any incriminating evidence on her when she was so certain she'd had nothing to do with Greg's death?

Are you sure? a little voice whispered in her head. *Are you positive you weren't there? Are you certain you didn't go to Greg's room, fight with him and lose your temper?*

She thought again of that night she'd gone to bed, only to awaken in the middle of the yard with no memory, no idea of how she'd gotten there.

Was that what had happened on the night of Greg's murder? She remembered driving to Walker's pond, still seething over Greg's threats to take Cody from her. Had her anger manifested itself in some form of sleep disturbance, causing her to not only walk in her sleep, but to kill in her sleep?

"No." She whispered the denial softly. There had to be another answer. There had to be another killer. But who? And why?

"Judge Billings is out for the afternoon," Richard said, his gaze capturing hers as he looked at her in the rearview mirror. "It looks like you won't be arraigned until sometime tomorrow."

"You mean I'll have to spend the night in jail?" She'd been so sure Matthew Curtis, the family lawyer, would be able to get her out of jail within hours.

Richard snorted. "You'll be lucky if all you spend is one night in jail. I imagine the prosecutor will request no bail. You'll probably be in jail until the day they transfer you to prison."

His words echoed in Abby's head, sending cold chills racing up her spine. Prison. Suddenly the total reality of her situation hit home. She could go to prison. Cody would grow up without her. His birthdays would pass without her presence, he'd grow into manhood and she wouldn't be there to see each rite of passage. With these horrifying thoughts spinning in her head, Abby leaned her head against the seat and silently sobbed.

WHEN THE PATROL CAR had disappeared from sight, Luke walked into the house. He should feel good. He should be euphoric. This was exactly what he'd wanted. Justice. So why did his heart feel so heavy? Why was he plagued by doubts?

Maybe his doubts grew from the haunted look in Abby's eyes as they'd clicked the handcuffs around her wrists. Or perhaps his doubts found their seeds in the tears that had trekked down her cheeks as the officers had led her to the patrol car.

Dammit. Never had a woman so confused him.

He'd come to the ranch certain of his facts, intending to make Abby ease up on Greg, make her allow him access to his son. But before he could do that, Greg was killed and all the rules—all his facts—changed.

He wanted Greg's murderer to go to jail, wanted somebody to pay for that crime. But was Abby guilty? Initially he'd been so certain. However, somehow in the space of the past couple of days, he'd lost the luxury of his certainty.

He looked at his watch, wondering what time Cody would return from his little friend's house. Already he regretted his promise to Abby to watch over the kid until Abby returned this evening or Belinda came home the next day. Maybe Maria would return from her sister's soon, he thought hopefully. What in the hell did he know about kids?

Deciding the best thing to do was to keep himself occupied while he waited for Cody, Luke went into Abby's room where the officers had left behind a mess.

What had Richard Helstrom seen on Abby's blouse that had prompted her arrest? The question played in his mind as he rehung her clothes in the closet. Blood? Surely if Abby had killed Greg, she wouldn't have been foolish enough to hang a bloody blouse back in her closet. Abby might be many things, but she wasn't stupid.

After finishing the closet, he moved on to the bed, where the police officers had dumped the contents of the drawers. As he folded the clothes and put them away, his gaze took in the bedroom, unsurprised to find it unfrilly, but nonetheless quite feminine.

The dresser was heavy cherrywood; the bed had a matching antique headboard. The bright yellow bedspread and matching curtains added a cheerful warmth. Unlike most women, whose dressertops Luke suspected would be cluttered with perfumes and creams and jewelry, treasures from Cody decorated Abby's. A cast of a little hand, a self-portrait stick figure, a vase with dead wildflowers. It seemed that every gift Cody might have made or bought for his mother over his brief life was here, a testimony to the mother-son love between the two.

Luke frowned, fighting a feeling that he was invading her privacy as he shoved her underthings into their proper drawer. His head filled with a vision of Abby in the cotton briefs and bras. The white fabric would look exotic against her smooth, tanned skin. The clothing smelled like her, a sweet fragrance that eddied in the air of the room.

"Hey, Mom, I'm home." The slam of the front door punctuated Cody's announcement. Luke put the last of the garments away, then hurried out of the bedroom. He met Cody in the hall.

"Hi, Luke. What are you doing here?" he asked. "Where's my mom?"

Abby hadn't told Luke what to tell Cody about her absence. "She's not here. I'm sort of baby-sitting you until she gets home. Why don't we go into the kitchen?" Luke said as he tried to figure out exactly how much to tell the boy about Abby's arrest.

Cody scowled at him. "Cowboys don't have baby-sitters," he protested.

"Six-year-old cowboys do," Luke countered.

"Can I have a cookie?" Cody asked once they were in the kitchen.

Luke hesitated. Only two minutes on the job and already he felt inundated with the task of making decisions. "Okay," he agreed, deciding a cookie couldn't hurt.

He watched as Cody grabbed a cookie from the jar on the countertop, then went to the refrigerator to pour himself a glass of milk. "You want some?" he asked.

Luke shook his head. He wasn't sure what he wanted or needed. Maybe a good, stiff drink? A long vacation? Somehow he knew cookies and milk wouldn't help a bit. "Sit down, Cody," he finally said, gesturing to the chair at the table across from him.

Cody carried his milk and cookie to the table, then sat down, looking at Luke curiously. "Is something wrong?" he asked. His blue eyes darkened. "Is my mom okay?"

Luke decided to opt for the truth, knowing that's probably what Abby would do. "You know somebody killed your father," he began. Cody nodded solemnly. "Well, the police think maybe your mom had something to do with it and they've taken her to the police station to talk to her about it."

Cody stared at him for a long moment, then sighed and took a bite of his cookie. "Boy, if those policemen think my mom hurt my dad, then they're really dumb." He rolled his eyes to emphasize his disgust at the very idea. "My mom wouldn't ever hurt anyone."

"It might take the police a little while to understand that," Luke explained. "And since neither your aunt Belinda nor Maria is here right now, it looks like I'll be taking care of you until your mom or your aunt or Maria return."

"Kind of like a stepdad, right?" Cody gazed at him slyly.

"No, kind of like a baby-sitter." Luke eyed the little boy curiously. "Besides, what do you know about stepdads?"

"I know I'm looking for one." Cody took a swig of his milk, giving himself a white mustache, before continuing. "When I was littler, I told my mom I wanted a new dad, you know, 'cause mine was never around. Mom explained to me that you can't just get new dads, that you can get stepdads. So, that's what I want."

Luke got up and grabbed a napkin, then thrust it to the boy. "Wipe your mouth," he instructed.

Cody grinned widely. "Now you sound like a stepdad," he exclaimed.

Luke had a feeling it was going to be a very long day.

"WHAT DO YOU WANT for dinner?" Luke asked Cody that evening. Once again they were in the kitchen after spending all afternoon working in the barn. They had exercised the horses, then cleaned out the stalls and put in fresh hay.

Cody had worked like a trouper, taking instructions from Luke and chattering about everything he felt important that had ever happened in his lifetime. Luke heard about his third birthday party, when he caught his first fish, how Bulldog had taught him to spit for distance.

Luke had listened with half an ear, his thoughts on Abby and what might be happening to her. Did she have a good lawyer? Would they set bail for her?

"Ice cream and popcorn." Cody's voice pulled Luke back to the present. It took him a moment to figure out what Cody was talking about. Dinner.

"I have a feeling your mother definitely wouldn't approve. How about hot dogs and beans? Now that's a real cowboy dinner." Besides, it was one of the few things Luke could cook.

Within minutes he had their supper ready and they sat at the table to eat. As they ate, Luke found himself wishing Cody was just a little older, that he could ask the boy questions about his mother, his dead father, get answers to the puzzles that suddenly plagued Luke's thoughts.

What if Abby hadn't killed Greg? That meant there was still a killer loose, a killer who for some reason wanted to implicate Abby, someone who had access to the branding irons.

"Tell me something about the men who work here." He figured the boy, in his innocence and friendliness, might know something that adults wouldn't know about the men working for his mother.

"Like what?" Cody asked as he added more catsup to his hot dog.

"You like the men who work for your mom?"

Cody shrugged. "Some of them. Bulldog is my best friend, and Roger is sort of nice."

Luke nodded. Roger Eaton had a ready smile and an easy friendliness. "What about Rusty?"

"He's okay, 'cept he's always telling me kids should be seen and not heard."

"Is there any of the men that your mom has had trouble with?"

Cody's eyes darkened. "Billy and Mom sometimes yell at each other."

Luke thought of the sullen, alcoholic man. There had obviously been some bad blood between Billy and Abby before she'd fired him. Had it been enough for Billy to kill Greg Foxwood and then frame Abby?

He rubbed his forehead, wondering why in the hell he found himself working hard to come up with another suspect. Everything pointed to Abby. She wouldn't have been arrested had the evidence not distinctly pointed to her culpability. Although his head said to leave things alone, that the odds were good that Abby was the guilty party, his heart entertained a disturbing doubt.

Frowning, he bid Cody to finish his meal, eager to put the kid to bed. He didn't know why he'd promised to look after him to begin with. Something about Abby Connor had him doing things, thinking things, completely out of character, and he didn't like it. He didn't like it one little bit.

Later in the evening, Luke watched from the doorway as Cody crawled into bed. "Will my mom be home tomorrow?" Cody asked, his eyes half cast with sleepiness.

Luke hesitated, not wanting to make unrealistic

promises. "I'm not sure. But your aunt Belinda should be back sometime tomorrow."

"Wanna see my letters from my dad?" Cody asked. Before Luke could answer, Cody leaned over and pulled a handful of paper from the drawer next to the bed.

Drawn by curiosity, despite his reluctance, Luke walked across the room and sat on the edge of Cody's bed. Three letters in six years. Luke had expected more.

The familiar handwriting on the pieces of paper shot an arrow of grief through Luke, grief he swallowed before allowing it to consume him.

The creases in the letters were worn, attesting to the fact that the letters had been read and reread many times. "He always promised to come and see me, but he never came," Cody said softly, and in Cody's voice Luke heard the resounding sorrow of broken promises, the shattered faith of a little boy.

Once again Luke's doubts about Abby's guilt exploded in his mind. Luke had been told lies and he'd believed them as truths. That's what had brought him out here. It had been lies that had made him leave his home in Chicago and travel here.

Had anything he'd been told been true? And if everything he had been told was a lie, then Abby Connor wasn't a cold, ruthless witch; it was possible she was merely a victim.

Cody yawned tiredly and Luke handed him the letters. "You'd better put these away before you fall asleep." Luke watched as the little boy carefully placed the letters into the drawer where he'd initially gotten them. "My mom says my dad was a real cow-boy, but I don't think he was. I think he was just a pretend one."

"Why do you say that?"

Cody frowned thoughtfully. "'Cause if he'd been a real cowboy, he would have stayed with me and my mom. He wouldn't have left us alone when I was a baby."

Again in Cody's wistful voice Luke heard the whisper of little-boy longing. He didn't want to be moved by it, didn't want to be vulnerable to caring about Cody.

Cody was obviously hungry for a father figure, a man who deserved to be loved and looked up to. Cody needed a hero, a real cowboy, and Luke certainly wasn't the man.

Luke was here under false pretenses. Real cowboys didn't lie, and nearly every word out of Luke's mouth since he'd arrived had been a lie. Real cowboys lived up to their commitments, honored their vows, and Luke had failed at that long ago.

Cody was looking for a hero, and Luke wasn't a hero. In fact, Luke had a feeling that before every-thing was said and done, Cody would hate him...because before this was all over, he had a feel-ing he would be just another man who made Abby cry.

Chapter Seven

Bert Manigan had the personality of a pit bull. Aggressive, tenacious and more than a little obnoxious, he also enjoyed a reputation as one of the best lawyers in the state of Wyoming.

Although Abby had never met the man, Junior had arranged for Bert to meet Abby an hour before she was set to be arraigned. Abby's family lawyer had confessed to Abby that he couldn't do anything for her in a criminal trial, so Junior had stepped in and arranged things for her.

Bert told her his fee, an amount that stole her breath away, but after spending a night in the jail cell, Abby would have paid him with her soul if he could get her out and back to the ranch with Cody.

"The state's case is weak," Bert said. "Mostly circumstantial. The threats you made, no alibi for the time of the murder, and the missing button from your blouse."

"The missing button?"

"Apparently a button was found beneath Greg Foxwood's body. The button came off your blouse."

How was that possible? Fear fluttered through Abby's stomach. How was it possible for her button to be beneath Greg unless...unless she'd been there?

As Bert went through the arraignment procedure, explaining everything to Abby, cautioning her to let him do the talking, she wondered if she should tell him about the night she awoke on the lawn. The phone call she'd thought was from Greg. She decided against telling him, not wanting to muddy the waters with things she didn't understand. Besides, the phone call was obviously a prank, and the other event had merely been a single incident of stress-induced sleep-walking.

"That should do it," Bert said, rising from the conference table where they'd been seated. "I'll see you in court in less than an hour."

"Mr. Manigan? You never asked me if I did it."

Bert grinned. "I don't want to know. Guilt or innocence, it's all the same to me. My job is to see you don't get convicted and I'm damn good at my job."

An hour later Abby pleaded not guilty to the charge of second-degree murder and Bert argued for a reasonable bail to be set. Less than two hours later she walked out of the jail, a free woman until the date of her trial set in six weeks' time.

Six weeks of freedom. Six weeks to find a killer, Abby thought as Junior drove her back to the ranch. And if they didn't find a reasonable doubt that she didn't kill Greg, she'd go to prison for years. Cody would grow up without a mother and the ranch would be lost to future generations of Connors.

She nearly laughed aloud at this thought. The ranch was probably already lost. With her bail and Bert

Manigan's fee, she'd never manage to pull the ranch out of the red.

"Abby, I'm sorry." Junior finally broke the silence that had reigned during their drive.

"For what? For doing your job?" She offered him a forgiving smile. "Junior, I don't blame you for this mess. The problem is, I don't know who to blame."

"Abby, I've been thinking long and hard about this. If you had nothing to do with Greg's death, then the murderer has to be somebody at your ranch."

Abby sighed. "I know. I've come to the same conclusion." She thought of the people at the ranch, her family, the workers whom she'd come to depend on and trust. "And it has to be somebody who not only has access to the barn, but to the house, as well. I'm telling you, Junior, somebody pulled that button from my blouse to intentionally incriminate me." She shivered at the very thought. Who at the ranch hated her enough to do such a thing? Who would want to see her in prison for a crime she didn't commit?

"What about that new fellow out at your ranch?" Junior asked.

"Luke?" Abby frowned thoughtfully. Her heart picked up its pace as she thought of the day he'd arrived. "What about him?" she asked. He'd arrived on the day that Greg had been murdered. Coincidence? Or something more ominous?

"What do you know about him?" Junior returned her question with his own.

Who was Luke Black? What did she really know about him? Nothing. Only the bits and pieces he'd shared with her, and they had been few and of little use in discerning his character or exactly what had brought him to her ranch.

"Not enough," she finally admitted. She thought of the shine on his boots, the new, raw calluses on his hands. Neither were in keeping with a seasoned ranch hand. So, who was he really and what had brought him to the ranch?

She shivered as a new thought entered her mind. What if Luke did have something to do with Greg's death? What if he had some sort of vendetta against the Connors, against her? She'd left him in charge of Cody. Dear God, she'd put her most precious possession right in his hands.

As Junior pulled up in front of the house, her heart pounded so loudly she was surprised the lawman couldn't hear it. "Thanks for the ride," she said as she flew from the car.

"Cody?" she yelled as she opened the front door.

"We're in the kitchen, Mom."

She nearly sobbed with relief at the sound of his voice. She entered the kitchen to see Cody at the table and Luke at the stove. "Luke is making pancakes," Cody exclaimed.

"So I see." She went over to her son, needing to touch him, hug him, reassure herself he was fine.

"Mom," he protested as she kissed his cheek.

"Maria is still gone?" Abby asked as she sank into a chair at the table.

"She called this morning, said her sister is doing better and she should be back by the end of the week," Luke replied as he removed pancakes from the griddle and placed them on a plate. "Want some?" As he placed the plate in front of Cody, his gaze lingered on her face searchingly. "You all right?"

"As right as I can be," she said, not wanting to say too much in front of Cody.

"Did they let you go?"

She shook her head. "I was charged and arraigned. I'm out on bail."

"What's bail?" Cody asked as he smothered his pancakes in syrup.

"Just grown-up stuff," Abby answered.

"Did the police find out who killed Dad?"

"No, son, they didn't. They're still looking." Abby hoped to hell her words were true. Hopefully Junior or some member of the police force was still investigating and hadn't quit because of her arrest.

"Coffee?" Luke asked.

"Please." She murmured her thanks as he set a cup in front of her, then poured himself one and joined them at the table. "I can't thank you enough for baby-sitting Cody for me."

"Don't say baby-sitting," Cody said with a mouthful of pancake and a scowl. "I'm not a baby."

As Cody ate, Luke and Abby kept their conversation light, but she could see the questions in his eyes, the need to know what had happened, how she'd fared in jail.

"Well, I'd better get out of here," Luke finally said after his second cup of coffee. "Rusty will be complaining about me being in here instead of out there earning my pay."

"If he complains, I'll take care of him. You've

more than earned your pay dealing with this little monster for a night." She ruffled Cody's hair, then stood to walk with Luke to the front door.

All her earlier questions and worries about him had disappeared. Had he wanted to harm her, he could have done so last night, with Cody.

"So what happens now?" Luke asked as they stepped out onto the front porch.

Abby wrapped her arms around herself despite the heat of the sun overhead. "My lawyer is coming by this evening and we're going to discuss defense strategy." She forced a smile. "He seems to think I need more than a proclamation of innocence to get me off."

"What else can you get?"

"I can find the real killer." Abby shivered and looked out to where the hired help went about the business of keeping the ranch running. "Whoever killed Greg is out here, close to me, pretending to be a friend while setting me up."

"What makes you think that?"

"Nothing else makes any sense. Whoever killed Greg got into my closet and pulled a button off the blouse I wore the night of the murder. Whoever killed Greg used my branding iron as the weapon. Somebody wants me put away for a murder I didn't commit, and it's somebody on this ranch."

"So, how are you going to go about finding out who this someone is?" There was a touch of indulgent humor in his expression.

"I'm glad you find this amusing," she snapped. "I'm already about to lose this ranch, and if I don't do something, I'll probably spend the rest of my life in prison.''

"I'm sorry," he replied. "I don't mean to poke fun, but you aren't exactly Jessica Fletcher."

"No, I'm not." To her horror, tears burned at her eyes. "But I can't just sit around and do nothing." She swallowed hard, trying to control the tears, but failing. "I've never felt so frightened, or so alone."

He pulled her into his arms. For a moment, as tears splashed down her cheeks, she leaned into him. His T-shirt smelled of sunshine and strength, and for just a moment she allowed herself to be weak, allowed him to hold her up both physically and emotionally.

It felt so good. She felt as if she'd spent her lifetime alone and in these moments of allowing Luke to support her, she gave him her trust, a tiny piece of her heart.

"Is there anything I can do?" he asked when she finally moved out of his embrace.

She shook her head, then smiled. "You just did it." They both turned at the sound of a car approaching. "What now?" Abby sighed. At least it wasn't a police car, rather it was an expensive luxury model. Abby groaned. "Just what I need. Henry Carsworth."

"Who's Henry Carsworth?" Luke asked.

"A vulture," Abby replied as a squat, short man got out of the car. "Morning, Mr. Carsworth."

He tipped the hat that looked ridiculously small atop his big head. "Henry. I told you the other day to call me Henry." He flashed a grin almost as bright as the sparkle on the huge belt buckle he wore. "I figured after a night in jail you might be willing to talk turkey."

"A night in jail didn't change my mind, Mr. Carsworth. The ranch is not for sale."

Henry's grin didn't waver. He pulled a fat cigar from his pocket and lit it, his gaze going first to Abby, then to Luke, then back to Abby. "Now, now, let's not be hasty. Perhaps we can go inside where it's more private, you can listen to my offer, then make a decision."

"It doesn't matter what your offer is, my decision has already been made."

Henry placed a foot on the porch, displaying a custom-made snakeskin boot with a three-inch heel. "Be reasonable, Abby. You're in trouble, in big trouble. Way I hear it, all that's keeping this place afloat is your determination. Now you've got legal bills and a criminal case hanging over your head. What you going to leave that boy of yours if you go to prison? You're going to lose the ranch. Why not let me buy it, I'll give you a fair price, enough to pay your legal fees and still live a good life or put some in a trust fund for your kid."

Abby grimaced with annoyance. "Mr. Carsworth, this ranch is not for sale."

For the first time since his arrival his smile fell. He dropped the cigar to the ground and squashed it beneath his heel. "I'm going to own this ranch, Abby. I can either buy it now, or I can buy it later, when you're in prison. But, one way or the other, this ranch will be mine." He tipped his hat, then walked back to his car.

"That snake," Abby hissed beneath her breath.

"Who exactly is he?" Luke asked.

"He's a wealthy man from California who's a wanna-be."

"A wanna-be?"

"He wants to be a cowboy and he wants my ranch."

Luke gazed at the road, where the last stirring of dust from the car lingered in the air. "I wonder how badly he wants to own your ranch?"

"Why?"

Luke looked back at her. "I wonder if he wants it bad enough to frame you for murder?"

GUILTY OR INNOCENT? Those two words plagued Luke all day. They battled in his head, sparred in his heart. Could any woman be as good as Abby at radiating innocence and hiding guilt if it weren't true?

Luke had a feeling he was out of his depth. If he were smart, he'd head back to Chicago, back to his desk job and solitary life-style. If he were smart, he'd leave it to the authorities to decide Abby's guilt or innocence, allow the judicial process to either punish her or let her go. But, for the first time in his life, Luke didn't want to be smart.

He couldn't leave here without knowing exactly who was responsible for Greg's death. He leaned against the corral fence. Dammit, it had all been so clear when he'd left Chicago to travel out here. He'd been determined to straighten things out, to right past wrongs.

"You seem to be worming your way in real good with the boss lady."

Luke turned and grinned at Rusty. "She's an attractive woman, I'm a healthy man."

Rusty snorted. "If you're thinking you can weasel your way into owning a piece of this place by snuggling up to her, you'd better think again. That's what her first husband tried to do and look what it got him."

Luke looked at the old man sharply. "What do you mean? Are you saying Greg married Abby to get the ranch?"

Rusty shrugged. "I'm just an old fool, but that's the way it appeared to me. Abby's parents had just passed away, leaving her in charge. From the moment he arrived here, he honed in on her like a hawk to a rabbit. When she refused to put the place in his name, he left her."

"What kind of a boss is she?"

"Hard, but fair." Rusty rubbed his jaw thoughtfully. "That is until lately."

"What about lately?"

Rusty frowned and again stroked his whiskered jawline. "I don't know…lately she seems to be real absentminded, you know. Even before the murder, she seemed to have moments when I wasn't sure she was all there."

Luke sighed and ran a hand through his hair. "You got family, Rusty?"

"Had a wife and a little boy once. The wife took the boy and left me years ago. Never heard from her again."

Luke looked at him curiously. "What about your son?"

"He got in touch with me not long ago, had lots of questions I couldn't answer, seemed to need things I couldn't give him." Rusty sighed, the wearied sigh of an old man. "Ah, family…better off without them."

"So, who do you think killed Greg?"

Rusty ran a gnarled hand through his grizzled gray hair and his frown deepened. "Don't know for sure, but I can tell you one thing." He looked toward the house. "I saw her come home the night he was murdered. I heard she told the police she was out at Walker's pond, but when she drove in that night she came from the opposite direction. She came from the direction of town."

Luke frowned and also looked toward the house, more confused than ever. Was Abby an innocent victim of some conspiracy, or was she an evil, heartless woman who would do anything to protect what was hers?

"I'LL BE IN TOUCH later in the week," Bert Manigan said as he walked to the front door.

Abby nodded wearily. Midnight approached, and they had been talking since eight o'clock. Her mind whirled with all his proposed legal maneuvering, most of which she didn't understand. "Thanks, Bert."

He smiled. "Don't worry. If my investigator doesn't turn up something we can use in your defense, we'll ask for a continuance. We won't go to trial without a good defense plan."

Don't worry. She nearly laughed aloud at the words
as she closed and locked the door behind the lawyer.
How could she not worry? Her entire life was falling
apart.

At least for the moment things were in as much
control as they could possibly be. Colette and Hank
had called earlier, raving about their trip and how
much fun they were having. Abby hadn't told them
about her arrest, refusing to allow her own problems
to ruin their vacation.

Both Belinda and Cody were asleep and the house
was quiet. Abby had always enjoyed the peace and
tranquillity the house seemed to radiate when everyone else was in bed. As she changed into her nightgown, she thought of those nights long ago, when she
and her sisters were little and they would snuggle in
bed together and tell stories until their mother would
come in and send them all to their own rooms.

Abby had always been the best storyteller, able to
make up ghost stories that had made her sisters squeal
in terror. But nothing had prepared her for the horror
story now taking place in her life.

She went into the kitchen and made herself a cup
of hot cocoa, then sat at the table and listened to the
familiar settling of the house, the soft tick-tock of the
kitchen clock, all the sounds of home that warmed
her heart as effectively as the cocoa warmed her in-
sides.

Somehow, someway she had to hang on to the
ranch. If she could just make it through the trial, if
they could survive until fall, then there would be cattle to sell, and hopefully beef prices would be good.

The problem was she wasn't sure they could survive until fall.

Earlier that afternoon she'd received two phone calls from stores in town who'd requested payments on her overdue accounts. What frightened Abby was that she had been certain she'd paid the bills. The checks had been missing from her checkbook, but both store managers had insisted they had received no payments.

A call to the bank had only raised Abby's apprehension. She'd been routed to the bank vice president, who explained that he could give her no information on her account as the computer was down and in any case the police had a current printout of her account information.

She'd asked Bert what the ranch bank account could possibly have to do with Greg's murder, and he'd told her he'd find out what he could.

She'd just finished her second cup of cocoa when the phone rang. Immediately her heart leapt with fear. It was after midnight. Ringing phones this late at night never brought good news. The last late call she'd received had been from her dead ex-husband. As the phone rang again she flew into action. She opened first one cabinet drawer, then another, sighing in relief as she found what she sought. Cody's tape recorder. Praying there was a tape inside, hoping the batteries were still good, she clicked it on and held it to the phone earpiece as she answered.

"Hello?"

"It's me."

She gasped, the familiar voice shattering her composure.

"Greg."

"No, it isn't," she protested. "Greg is dead. Who is this? Why are you doing this to me?" She recognized the hysteria in her voice at the same time she heard the soft click indicating that whoever it was had hung up.

She replaced the receiver in the cradle, her hand violently trembling. She shut off the tape recorder and fought against the cold chill of hysteria.

Logically, she knew it had to be some kind of prank, but how? It was Greg's voice. There was no doubt in her mind. And why...why would somebody play such a terrible trick on her?

Suddenly the kitchen felt stifling. She walked through the living room, then stepped out onto the front porch. The warm night air chased the chill from the surface of her skin, but couldn't touch the frigid core of fear deep within her.

She took a deep breath, fighting against a slight dizziness. Leaning against the railing, she looked up at the moon overhead, a sliver of overripe honeydew melon. As she watched, the moon appeared to melt and reshape, taking on a new form...Greg's face. He glowered down at her, a malevolent omnipotent being where the moon had once been.

Fear shimmied up Abby's spine as he stared down at her, his eyes craters of anger, of rage.

With a small cry of anguish, Abby left the porch, seeking a hiding place from his ominous glare. She raced across the lawn, passed the corral where the horses nickered and danced in surprise as she flew by.

She ran in a frenzy, the world suddenly filled with threatening sights and sounds. The night air blew on the nape of her neck like the hot breath of a pursuing demon. A coyote howled in the distance, as if bidding her to run faster...faster.

She finally collapsed beneath the dense foliage of the massive ancient oak she and her sisters called the dragon tree. The thick, leaf-laden branches effectively hid the luminous face of her dead ex-husband from her view. She felt safe here. She'd always felt safe within the shadows of the dragon tree. Growing up, she and her sisters had often played here, spinning fantasies of love and happily-ever-afters.

Tears welled in her eyes as she remembered those carefree times, when everything seemed possible and hopes were wishes yet to be fulfilled. She squeezed her eyes tightly closed, focusing on those memories of youth.

Slowly her fear ebbed and peace stole through her. Colors danced in her head and the night breeze caressed her with a lover's fingers of warmth. As the wind stirred the leaves on the tree, Abby knew it was the sound of the dragon breathing...the dragon trapped in the tree.

"If I let the dragon go, he'll grant me a wish," she whispered aloud. "And I'll wish that he take Greg's face from the sky and bury it in the ground where he can't look down on me."

She stood and stared up the massive trunk. Placing a hand on the wood, she could feel the vibration of life pulsing within. At the top, trapped in the dense leaves, lived the dragon. She could see his haunted eyes gazing down at her, silently pleading with her to help him, free him.

She grabbed a sturdy branch, her bare feet scrambling to find leverage as she pulled herself up. As she looked down, the ground swam with swirling colors and again a wave of dizziness swept through her. She had to go up. The heart of the dragon was in the top of the tree. She stood and grabbed the branch over her head, intent on climbing up…up….

Chapter Eight

Luke wasn't sure what awakened him. For a moment he remained in his bed, unmoving, listening to the sounds of the other men in the room sleeping.

He waited for sleep to overtake him once again, but restless energy chased further slumber away. The bunkhouse felt oppressive, hot, and he decided a breath of fresh air was in order.

Silently, like a thief in the night, he slipped into his jeans and pulled on his boots, then left the bunkhouse. Outside, the moon shone brightly, illuminating the landscape and spilling down silvery light.

He sat on the bench outside the bunkhouse, breathing in deeply of the sweet-scented, warm night air. Funny, he hadn't missed Chicago at all since he'd been here. At another time, in other circumstances, he would have looked on his time at the ranch as the vacation he'd always wanted to take.

Although various muscles ached and throbbed, the physical work felt good, reminding him that at one time he'd dreamed of owning or working on a ranch.

He leaned his head against the rough exterior of the bunkhouse, his mind whirling with thoughts of

Abby. He remembered now what had awakened him. A dream.

In his dream he'd been with Abby in her bedroom. She'd been on the bed, clad in a revealing silk nightgown the color of a blush. She'd raised her arms, beckoning him toward her. Her eyes had been lit with a fire that threatened to consume him, and he'd wanted to be consumed. As he joined her on the bed, she pulled a branding iron from beneath her pillow and raised it over him. That's when he'd awakened.

He rubbed his eyes tiredly, the dream lingering in his head. Had it been his subconscious attempting to show him truth, or merely his own doubts manifested in his dreams?

Looking out on the brilliantly lit landscape, he tried to shove away the memory of his dream. It was difficult to imagine someone as outwardly beautiful as Abby being capable of killing a man, but Luke knew beauty often masked weakness and evil. Still, he'd always believed the adage that the eyes were the windows to the soul, and in the depths of Abby's blue eyes he saw nothing to indicate any hint of a dark core. Confusion boiled inside him, making it impossible to figure out exactly what he felt about Abby Connor. He couldn't decide if she was innocent or guilty as conflicting beliefs constantly barraged him.

He sighed in frustration as he gazed toward the old oak tree standing on a nearby rise. He frowned, his gaze captured by something foreign in the branches.

He narrowed his eyes, focused on the upper branches of the tree where a swatch of white material gleamed amid the greenery. "What the hell?" he murmured, rising from the bench. Somebody was in the tree.

He approached stealthily, unsure who it was, what they might be doing. He stuck to the shadows as he worked his way to the base of the large oak. Once there, he realized the someone in the tree was Abby.

She made no attempt to be quiet. He could hear her soft muttering and the branches and leaves shook as she advanced farther and farther up.

"Abby?"

She squealed in surprise and stood still, as if attempting to hide from him.

"Abby, what are you doing up there?"

"Go away. I've got to get to the dragon. If I let him go, he'll make Greg go away."

Luke frowned, unable to make sense from her words. "Abby, come down and talk to me." He held his breath as she missed a step and frantically clung to the trunk. She was high enough that if she fell, she could be seriously harmed. Was it possible she was drunk?

"I have to get the dragon," she replied, her voice dreamy and soft.

"Come down and I'll help you get the dragon." Still Luke had no idea what she was talking about. All he knew was that she needed to get out of the damned tree before she fell and broke her neck.

"You'll help me?"

"I promise," Luke answered.

She hesitated a long moment, remaining still. "Can you make Greg go away?"

What in the hell was going on? "Of course I will."

He held his breath as she remained unmoving. "Come on, Abby. Come down and I'll take care of everything."

"Oh, yes. Yes, I'd like that."

As Luke watched, she began to descend. His heart filled his throat as he watched, afraid that with one misstep, one false move, she'd fall.

He didn't breathe again until her feet hit the ground. "What in the hell were you doing up there?" he asked, fear changing to anger now that she was safe.

She leaned against the tree trunk and gazed upward. "I told you. I was going to get the dragon. He's trapped in the tree and if I get him out, he'll make Greg stop looking at me."

Luke had heard the ranch hands refer to the misshapen oak as the dragon tree. He'd been told that the Connor girls had given it its name because of the way the foliage grew in the shape of the mythical beast. "Abby, there's no dragon in the tree and Greg is dead."

She looked at him, and in her eyes he saw the haze of unreality. "There's no dragon?" She took a step closer to him. He smelled no alcohol, but she acted like a woman under the influence of something. Her glazed eyes shimmered with tears and her mouth trembled. "Then who will make Greg go away and leave me alone? He calls me on the phone and he's looking at me right now."

Luke's heart thudded as he heard the singsong quality in her voice. "Where is he? Where's Greg now?" he asked.

She pointed up. "He's so angry. See how he glares?"

Luke directed his gaze to where she indicated. "Abby, that's just the moon."

She looked at him in surprise, then back up to the lunar light. "Oh. It is. It is just the moon." She laughed, a low, throaty sound that instantly shot through Luke like a bolt of electricity. "Oh, Luke, it's just the moon." She stepped toward him and wrapped her arms around his neck. She laughed again, her breath warm and sweet in the hollow of his neck. "It's just the silly old moon."

Despite his confusion with her mood and her actions, in spite of his uncertainty over her guilt or innocence, his body responded to her closeness. It was obvious to him she wore little or no underclothing beneath the light cotton nightgown. He could feel not only her body heat but also the press of her breasts and the length of her long legs against him.

"Abby, it's the middle of the night," he said, struggling to keep his body's response under control.

"Yes. I love the night, don't you?" She spun out of his arms, a wraith in the silvery spill of the moon. She held her arms out at her sides and twirled, her nightgown billowing from her slender shape. "I've always loved the night. I used to sneak out of the house when I was a little girl and sit and dream in the moonlight."

"Abby, let's go inside." Luke didn't know what was going on with her, but he knew something wasn't right. The distance in her eyes, the slow rhythm of her speech, the almost dreamlike fluidity of her movements told him something definitely wasn't right.

"No." She stopped her twirling. "It's too beautiful out here to go in." She approached him and placed a hand against his cheek. "Stay with me out here, Luke. Stay and dream with me under the moonlight."

Before he could protest, before he even knew her intention, she leaned into him and placed her lips on his. Her mouth was warm and open to him, shooting him from confusion to full-blown arousal in an instant.

She gave him no chance to catch his breath, no opportunity to swim against the tides of desire that engulfed him. Instead she pulled him in deeper, tangling her hands in his hair as she pressed herself intimately against him.

"Oh, Luke..." she moaned against his mouth. "Hold me, Luke. Hold me close and keep me safe. I'm so tired of being alone."

"Abby—"

"Make love to me here...now." Her hands left his hair and moved down his bare back, igniting fire as they caressed.

Her words sent a frenzy of need through him. How easy it would be to give in to her. His body throbbed with the desire her touch, her kiss, stirred. Visions filled his head, erotic visions of the two of them making love in the soft, sweet-smelling grass beneath the dragon tree.

He wanted to lose himself in her, momentarily stop his agonizing doubts and the more insidious pieces of grief that haunted him. He wanted to stop thinking and instead focus only on physical sensations of pleasure.

How easy it would be to shove aside his hesitation, ignore the hazy unfocus of her eyes, all the signs that told him she wasn't in her right mind. How easy it would be to do exactly what she bid and make love to her despite the fact that he had a feeling she really didn't know what she was doing.

How he wished he were a different kind of man, but he wasn't. When and if he made love to Abby, he wanted her to know each and every moment of that act. Besides, his ultimate goal was to make her trust him, and how could she trust a man who took advantage of her by making love to her when she was out of her mind?

"Come on, Abby. Let's go back to the house." He tried to unwind her arms from around his neck, but she fought him.

"No, please, Luke. I've been so frightened, so alone. Don't leave me."

"I won't, but let's go back into the house where we'll be more comfortable."

She looked up at him, her eyes luminous. "And you'll stay with me? You won't leave me alone and let Greg call me again?"

Luke had no idea what she was talking about, but recognized that her fear was genuine and the only way to get her back into the house was to assure her. "I'll stay with you and make sure Greg doesn't bother you."

He saw her trust in him shining in her eyes, and for a moment his conscience prickled uncomfortably.

He was here under false pretenses, determined to see her in jail if she were guilty of murder. He'd lied to her about everything that mattered and the vulnerability she exposed haunted him.

Taking her hand, he willfully silenced his conscience. The sin of deceit was far less weighty than the sin of murder.

She fell quiet as he led her into the dark house. By the time they entered her bedroom and he closed the door behind them, she seemed to be in a near stupor.

He turned on the bedside lamp and pulled down the blankets on the bed. She immediately crawled in. "Stay with me," she said as he started to move away from the bed. This time in her eyes he saw no passion, no flame of desire, but rather the whisper of fear. "Please...don't leave me by myself." It was as if the rational side of Abby fought to surface through the craziness.

He couldn't leave...that raw edge of fear in her eyes caused a nebulous hint of compassion to eddy inside him. He sank down on the edge of her bed. "I'll stay right here," he assured her.

"And you'll keep Greg away? You'll make him stop calling me?" Her eyelids drifted heavily and she blinked several times to remain focused on him.

"Don't worry, nobody is going to bother you." He pulled the sheet up around her neck, then ran his palm across her forehead. Perhaps a fever was responsible for her delusional state. But her skin was cool beneath his touch. "Abby, did you take some medicine tonight or perhaps have a few drinks?"

"No, I didn't take medicine, I'm not sick, and I don't drink. I'm just tired...so tired..."

As he watched, her eyelids closed and her breathing deepened and he knew she was out. He frowned thoughtfully and stared at her.

He knew he should go back to the bunkhouse and salvage what was left of the night, but he was reluctant to leave her alone. What if she awakened and once again decided to climb up the dragon tree? What if she decided to do something else even more dangerous?

He pulled up a chair next to the bed and sat, studying her features. She definitely hadn't been herself, and appeared to be in some sort of unstable mental fugue. All her talk of phone calls from Greg and releasing the dragon imprisoned in the tree had indicated a woman not in touch with reality.

Remembering Rusty's words, the old man's concerns about Abby's mental state, Luke frowned. Was it possible Abby was mentally ill? She had apparently suffered some frightening hallucinations if she'd believed the moon was Greg's face staring down at her.

She looked beautiful in sleep, making it difficult to imagine anything wrong with her. Her short blond hair framed her face with gentle curls and her long eyelashes splayed shadows on her cheeks. The pastel flowered bedsheets provided a perfect background for her tanned skin. Yes, she looked beautiful.

And yet he'd seen the confused reality shining in her eyes, heard the strain of dementia in her words.

Luke rubbed his forehead thoughtfully, still studying her sleeping features. Was it possible she was mentally ill? Suffering paranoid states, perhaps bouts of schizophrenia? He certainly wasn't a doctor, but he knew madness when he saw it, and that's exactly what he'd seen in Abby tonight.

His heart thudded slowly, sending icy blood through him. Had Abby killed Greg while in one of these states? Was it possible she'd killed him and didn't even remember it?

ABBY FOUGHT HER WAY through her dreams to consciousness, having trouble separating sleep images from reality. She'd dreamed she'd been climbing the dragon tree and she'd dreamed she'd been kissing Luke. She wasn't sure which had been more disturbing. The images were jumbled in her head, unclear as dreams often were, yet strangely vivid at the same time.

She stretched against the sheets, reassured by the familiar comfort of her own bed. With her eyes still closed, she reached up and shoved a curl off her forehead, then frowned as she encountered something alien in her hair.

She pulled it from her hair and opened her eyes, staring at it in confusion. A twig. A twig from an oak tree...the dragon tree.

"Good morning."

Abby jumped at the voice and rolled over to see Luke slumped in a chair next to the bed. "What are you doing in here?" she asked as she pulled the sheets more firmly around her.

He sat up, his bare chest painted gold by the bright sunshine streaming through the windows. "You

NO COST! NO OBLIGATION TO BUY! NO PURCHASE NECESSARY!

PLAY "LUCKY 7" AND GET FIVE FREE GIFTS

HOW TO PLAY:

1. With a coin, carefully scratch off the silver box at the right. Then check the claim chart to see what we have for you—FREE BOOKS and a gift—ALL YOURS! ALL FREE!

2. Send back this card and you'll receive brand-new Harlequin Intrigue® novels. These books have a cover price of $3.75 each, but they are yours to keep absolutely free.

3. There's no catch. You're under no obligation to buy anything. We charge nothing—ZERO—for your first shipment. And you don't have to make any minimum number of purchases—not even one!

4. The fact is thousands of readers enjoy receiving books by mail from the Harlequin Reader Service®. They like the convenience of home delivery…they like getting the best new novels BEFORE they're available in stores…and they love our discount prices!

5. We hope that after receiving your free books you'll want to remain a subscriber. But the choice is yours—to continue or cancel, anytime at all! So why not take us up on our invitation, with no risk of any kind. You'll be glad you did!

You'll love this plush, cuddly Teddy Bear, an adorable accessory for your dressing table, bookcase or desk. Measuring 5½" tall, he's soft and brown and has a bright red ribbon around his neck—he's completely captivating! And he's yours absolutely free, when you accept this no-risk offer!

DETACH AND MAIL CARD TODAY

THE HARLEQUIN READER SERVICE®: HERE'S HOW IT WORKS

Accepting free books places you under no obligation to buy anything. You may keep the books and gift and return the shipping statement marked "cancel". If you do not cancel, about a month later we'll send you 4 additional novels, and bill you just $2.94 each plus 25¢ delivery per book and applicable sales tax, if any.* That's the complete price–and compared to cover prices of $3.75 each–quite a bargain! You may cancel at any time, but if you choose to continue, every month we'll send you 4 more books, which you may either purchase at the discount price...or return to us and cancel your subscription.

*Terms and prices subject to change without notice. Sales tax applicable in N.Y.

BUSINESS REPLY MAIL
FIRST-CLASS MAIL   PERMIT NO. 717   BUFFALO, NY

POSTAGE WILL BE PAID BY ADDRESSEE

HARLEQUIN READER SERVICE
3010 WALDEN AVE
PO BOX 1867
BUFFALO NY 14240-9952

NO POSTAGE
NECESSARY
IF MAILED
IN THE
UNITED STATES

If offer card is missing, write to: Harlequin Reader Service, 3010 Walden Ave., P.O. Box 1867, Buffalo, NY 14240-1867 wouldn't let me leave last night. You begged me to stay here with you.''

''Last night?'' Abby frowned, trying to remember what had happened the night before, why she would have begged Luke to sleep in her room.

He'd obviously made himself at home. The second pillow from her bed rested behind his neck and he was not only shirtless, but several buttons on his jeans had been undone apparently for sleeping comfort. She flushed at the utter maleness of him, then thought again of what he'd just told her. She'd begged him to stay with her? When? Dear God, what had happened last night?

Fear jolted through her, a fear so deep, so dark, for a moment she couldn't speak. It had happened again. Just like the night she'd found herself in the middle of the lawn. The fear intensified as she remembered something else...the phone call from Greg. She looked at Luke, her heart pounding frantically. ''What happened last night?'' she finally asked, her mouth dry from her fear.

He sat up straighter in the chair and the pillow fell to the floor. ''I woke up just after midnight and went outside to get a breath of fresh air.'' He raked a hand through his disheveled hair, somehow managing only to look more attractive with his hair all askew. ''That's when I saw you in the dragon tree.''

''In the tree?'' Abby echoed softly, fighting a wave of profound despair.

Luke moved from his chair to the edge of the bed, his dark gaze somber. ''You were muttering about phone calls from Greg and releasing the dragon.''

Abby sat up and pulled her knees to her chest. So her crazy dreams had not been dreams at all. She really had climbed the dragon tree and she had no memory of it except for the flirting whispers of her dreams. "Oh, God. Luke, what's happening to me?"

"You don't remember anything from last night?"

She wrapped her arms around her knees, wishing she could curl up and disappear. "Vaguely...a few images, but I...I thought they were dreams." She looked at him, wondering how far she could trust him. She needed desperately to talk to someone, to share her fears. Someplace deep inside her wanted to be able to trust him.

As crazy as it seemed, in the short time they'd spent together she realized her heart had already built up a trust of him. "This has happened before," she finally confessed.

Luke's eyes narrowed. "When? How often?"

Abby sighed, hoping she wasn't making a mistake by telling him. "Just once that I know of...a couple nights ago. I woke up and found myself lying in the middle of the yard. I didn't know how I'd gotten there or where I'd been." She drew a deep, trembling breath. "I don't understand what's happening to me and it frightens me."

"Whew." He raked a hand through his hair once again. She knew she'd thrown him, troubled him, and that only made her own fear increase. "Why don't I go make some coffee and we can try to figure out what's going on?" he suggested.

Abby nodded and looked at the clock next to her bed. Almost nine o'clock. Panic swept through her.

"I had no idea it was so late. Where's Cody? He never sleeps this late."

"Relax," Luke replied as he stood. "Belinda came in earlier. She was pretty shocked to find me in here. I told her you'd been sick last night. She took Cody into town so you could rest today."

"No amount of rest is going to make me feel better about whatever is happening to me."

Luke hesitated at the door. He looked as if he were about to say something, then changed his mind. "I'll make the coffee," he finally said, then disappeared down the hallway.

For a long moment Abby remained unmoving, numbed by the fact that she'd experienced another inexplicable mental fugue. What was happening to her? Why was this happening to her?

Was she mentally ill? She didn't think there'd been any history of mental illness in her family. She frowned, remembering a night long ago when three girls had made a vow beneath the dragon tree...a vow never to discover which one of them was adopted.

There had been no mental illness in the Connor family background, but what if Abby wasn't truly a Connor? What if she had been adopted and her real mother now resided someplace in a mental hospital?

She pulled herself out of bed, refusing to dwell on these particular thoughts. Besides, it didn't matter whether she was adopted or not, didn't matter if her family history included every mental illness known to man, none of that information helped her with what she was going through now.

In the bathroom, she washed her face and brushed

her teeth, then stared at her reflection in the mirror. Fear darkened her eyes, and faint purple smudges beneath attested to too many nights with too little sleep. She looked tired and frightened. She felt exactly how she looked.

Was she the adopted one? Again the disturbing thought intruded. Was her real mother not dead and buried in the family cemetery, but rather institutionalized in an insane asylum? Had she suffered these same sort of blackouts and been put away for her own safety? For the safety of others? Again she shoved away these horrifying thoughts.

She picked up her hairbrush and ran it through her hair, frowning as she dislodged another piece of twig. She'd climbed the dragon tree last night. Madness. Sheer madness.

Smelling the scent of fresh-brewed coffee, she grabbed a robe from the hook on the bathroom door and pulled it on over her nightgown. With the robe firmly belted around her waist, she left the bathroom and went into the kitchen.

Luke stood at the door, staring out into the distance. His broad, tanned back caused a flutter of memory to ripple through Abby's mind. She'd touched his back last night. She'd stroked her hands up and down his warm flesh, felt the strength in his sleek muscles. What else had she done? What had they done?

She cleared her throat and he whirled around. For a moment his gaze burned into hers, fired with an intimacy that again made her worry about what had happened between them the night before. She had to know. "Luke...last night...did we..." Her voice trailed off as her face burned.

"Did we make love?" He walked toward her, stopping mere inches from where she stood. "Is that what you want to know?"

She nodded. She could feel the heat emanating from his bare chest, fought an urge to reach out and lose herself in his heat.

He touched her mouth with his index finger, tracing her full bottom lip softly, sensuously. "No, Abby. We didn't make love last night." He took a step closer to her, so close his chest touched the tips of her breasts. "When I make love to you, it won't be an experience you so easily forget." He dropped his hand and stepped back from her. "Sit down, I'll pour you a cup of coffee."

Dazed by the sensual heat his touch had evoked, she moved to the kitchen table and sank onto a chair. She watched as he maneuvered the kitchen with ease, finding cups in the appropriate cabinet and pouring the coffee with an efficiency of movement. He set a cup in front of her and joined her at the table.

For a moment neither of them spoke, but instead sipped the coffee as if each needed both the jolt of caffeine and the quiet to collect their thoughts.

The momentary flare of heat his touch had produced had waned. Abby curled her hands around her coffee cup, seeking the warmth of the drink, hoping it could seep into her bones and banish the chill that had taken up residence in her body.

"You okay?"

She looked up to meet his gaze, oddly comforted by the familiar darkness. "Not really, but I'm better."

He smiled. "Everything seems better with a cup of coffee." His smile faded. "Feel like talking?"

She shrugged. "About what?"

"About last night."

Again the chill renewed itself, shimmering up her back and raising goose bumps on her arms. "What's there to talk about? I don't remember it." She couldn't suppress a shiver.

"None of it?"

She frowned and stared into her coffee cup. "Vaguely...as if it were a dream...I've got pieces of memory."

"Tell me," he urged.

She closed her eyes and concentrated, trying to pull forth the images she'd thought had been dreams in her first edge of consciousness when awakening. "I remember climbing the tree. I needed something...I don't know—" She broke off in frustration.

"Go on. What else?"

"The moon. I remember the moon frightened me." She opened her eyes and looked at him, a flutter of warmth uncurling in the pit of her stomach. "And I remember kissing you."

He nodded, as if satisfied she'd remembered that. "When I first saw you up in the tree, I thought you might be drunk."

She shook her head. "I don't drink. I don't take drugs. That's what makes these blackouts all the more frightening."

Luke frowned and sipped his coffee. "So, what do you remember about last night before the blackout?"

"Bert Manigan, my lawyer, came by. He stayed until around midnight. After he left, the phone rang and it was Greg calling me again."

"Greg?"

"Oh, my gosh, I almost forgot." Adrenaline pumped through her as she remembered Cody's tape recorder. Racing to the phone she prayed the recorder had picked up the voice. At least it would be some small offer of proof that she wasn't completely losing her mind.

The tape recorder lay on the counter right next to the phone. She grabbed it and hurried back to the table. "A couple nights ago I got a late night phone call and it was Greg's voice on the other end of the line. Last night when the phone once again rang and it was so late at night, I grabbed this and taped it." She stared down at the tape recorder. "I just hope it worked."

"So do I." A slight edge of disbelief darkened his eyes.

Abby knew what he was thinking. That she was crazy, that it was impossible that Greg had called her, that the tape was probably blank and nothing more than another indication of her slipping sanity.

She rewound the tape, then pressed Play. Silence hissed on the tape. Despair shot through Abby. Had she imagined the phone call, Greg's voice? Was reality slipping further and further away from her?

She nearly sobbed in relief as her voice whispered "Hello?" on the tape.

"It's me. Greg." The male voice on the tape filled the kitchen.

Luke's coffee cup crashed to the floor, spewing coffee and shattering into a dozen pieces. He jumped out of his chair, staring at the tape recorder. When he looked at Abby, his eyes were dilated with shock.

Midnight Blue

with great unease every time I have to give out this information.

"Thank you," the lie grants. "I really appreciate this."

"No, dear, thank you."

She hung up the phone before she could ...

Chapter Nine

"Luke?" Abby stared at him, fear whispering through her at his reaction.

He took a deep breath, some of the shock leaving his expression. "I didn't expect to hear another voice. I thought maybe you just imagined the phone calls. It really surprised me. So, it sounds like Greg's voice?"

Abby nodded, relieved by his question. For a moment, seeing the shock on his face, she'd wondered if he knew Greg. But that was impossible. There was no way the two men could have met. "It doesn't just sound like him...it sounds exactly like him."

He leaned down and began picking up the pieces of the broken cup. "Sorry about this."

"Don't worry about it."

He finished with the cup then wet a paper towel and cleaned the coffee from the floor. When he was finished he rejoined her at the table. "So the call before this one...what did the caller say?"

She frowned. "About the same thing. Just, 'It's me. Greg.' But I'm telling you that's Greg's voice."

"Abby, no matter how much that voice sounds like

your ex-husband's, we both know it can't be him. Why would somebody be making calls like this to you?''

"Belinda thinks they're pranks…teenagers having fun at my expense.''

"Do you believe that?''

She shook her head, the coldness back inside her. "No. No teenager could imitate Greg's voice so well. I don't know who's responsible or why, and that's what frightens me so much.''

He reached out and covered one of her hands with his own. "We'll get to the bottom of this. Maybe you should get one of those Caller ID boxes.''

She smiled softly. "Unfortunately that technology isn't available around here yet. If they continue, I'll call the phone company and see if they'll put a tracer on the line.''

"I don't think you should wait for the calls to continue. Call the phone company today and get it done.''

Abby stood and carried her cup to the sink. She set down the cup, then leaned against the cabinet. "I feel like my entire life is so out of control. I'm waiting to be tried for murder, my dead ex-husband is calling me, and I'm having strange blackouts.''

Luke got up and walked over to where she stood. He placed his palm against her cheek. "And I have a feeling there's nothing you hate worse than not being in control.'' As he had done before, he traced the outline of her mouth with his index finger. "Sometimes letting go of control is a good thing,'' he said softly.

She knew she should move away from him, but she couldn't. His touch created a hungry fire inside her. He stepped closer, so close she could almost hear the pounding of his heart over the increased thudding of her own.

She knew she should move away because desire called to her, passion beckoned her, and she knew if she didn't step away from him, she'd do something crazy. And she knew by the look in his eyes that he wanted her. He wanted to make love to her.

She wanted that. She wanted to fall into his arms and let him obliterate everything else from her mind. She wanted to be able to trust him not only with her body, but with her heart, her soul. Something about Luke Black stirred her like no other man had in years. She wanted to trust him, and she wanted him to make love to her.

Her gaze still locked with his, as his finger once again traced the outline of her lips, she opened her mouth and drew his finger inside. His eyes flared and she heard his swift intake of breath.

As she saw the fires in his eyes, felt the tension that radiated through him, she knew they were about to cross a line that once crossed would forever change the complexities of their relationship. She would no longer just be his boss. He would no longer be one of her ranch hands. They would be lovers.

Why not? It was possible that in six weeks' time she'd be convicted of murder and put away in a prison for the rest of her life. Why not give herself a moment of memories?

She released his finger and moved into him, his

heat warming her through her robe and nightgown. She splayed her hands against the muscled plane of his chest and felt the taut tension that coiled through him at her caress.

With a muttered curse he captured her lips with his and pulled her more intimately against him, letting her know the extent of his arousal as his hips pressed against hers.

The hunger of his kiss gave her no time to change her mind, drove any lingering doubts out of her mind. Instead, a ravenous hunger grew in her, the need not only for the physical act of making love, but also for the connection of spirit with Luke.

She gasped as he untied her robe and pushed it aside. His mouth plied hers with heat as his hands sought her breasts, caressing through the thin cotton material of her nightgown.

His lips left hers, trailing down her jawline, lingering in the hollow of her throat. She dropped her head back, allowing him better access to the length of her neck as her fingers tangled in his thick hair.

He moaned softly against the pulse in the base of her throat. With apparent effort, he released his hold on her and stepped back. "Abby?"

She knew he was giving her an opportunity to stop right now, allowing her to make a rational decision. Her heart softened at his caring, but she didn't need to rethink anything. She knew what she wanted. She wanted him.

Without saying a word, she took his hand and led him out of the kitchen and to her bedroom, where the bed was still mussed and appeared to be awaiting them. She dropped his hand only long enough to shrug out of her robe, then pull her nightgown over her head, leaving her clad only in a pair of white cotton panties. She stretched out on the bed, feeling anxious and excited, knowing by allowing Luke to make love to her body, she gave him access to her heart.

As she watched, he took off his jeans. The sunlight streaming in the windows painted his body in lush tones, emphasizing his utterly male physique and turning Abby's bones to liquid fire. He joined her on the bed, immediately taking her in his arms.

Lost in his embrace, bewitched by his kisses and sweet caresses, Abby forgot all about everything else in her life. The worries about the ranch fell away, as did her fears of her own sanity and the terror of facing murder charges. She didn't think of the past, didn't worry about the future, but lived only in the moment...and Luke.

Luke's caresses were slow, languid, as if they had all of eternity to spend together. And how she wished they did. Abby had never felt so alive, as if her senses were heightened to extreme levels. His clean, masculine scent mingled with the sweet fresh air flowing in her window. The calluses on his palms only added to the erotic pleasure as he stroked them over her breasts.

His skin felt sleek and warm as they moved together in total abandon. Abby's heart thundered with each kiss, every caress. By the time his fingers slid down to encounter the barrier of her panties, she wanted him more than she'd ever wanted anything in her life.

With his gaze locked with hers, he slowly, sensually, pulled her panties off. When he touched her at the center of her being, tears of pleasure blurred her vision. He shifted positions and hovered over her for a moment, then slowly entered her.

As their bodies joined, she continued to look into his eyes. In their dark depths, she saw not only passion, but caring, tenderness...emotions that stirred her more deeply than any physical act could accomplish alone.

He moved, stroking urgency and need within her. As each thrust went deeper, became more powerful, she closed her eyes and gave herself completely to him.

ENVELOPED BY HER silken warmth, Luke lost himself. He forgot his reason for being here, lost track of his ultimate goal. All that mattered was this moment with Abby, making love to her.

He hadn't intended to take his seduction this far, and yet had been helpless to stop it once it had begun. He was aware that it had been his deceptions that had gotten him here, and yet there was nothing deceptive about his desire for her.

Her moans increased his urgency, feeding his hunger to staggering proportions. Engulfed in her heat, he found control near impossible...and yet he wanted the act to last forever.

Her moans increased in fervor as she met him thrust for thrust and as he felt her passion reaching its zenith, he whirled upward to his own. He whispered her name, wanting to look into her eyes as they went over the edge together.

As he looked into the midnight blue depths of her eyes, he saw the same wonder, the same awe he felt at their joining. He gasped, caught in a spiraling maelstrom that made any other thoughts impossible.

SOMETIME LATER they remained locked in each other's embrace. Their breathing slowed to a more normal rhythm, as did the pounding of their hearts. Luke leaned up on his elbow and gazed down at her, noting her sweet, swollen lips, the tousled hair and the flushed cheeks that were mute testimony to what they'd just shared.

She smiled, a touch of shyness to her expression. "Is this what you had in mind when you talked about letting go of control?"

He grinned. "You have to admit, there are merits to it." He traced a finger down her jawline. "Tell me something, when you were young and would sneak out of your house and dream while staring up at the moon, what kind of dreams did you have?"

Her eyes widened slightly. "How did you know I used to sneak out of the house at night?"

"You told me that last night. You wanted me to sit and dream with you in the moonlight. Tell me what you used to dream of."

She laughed with an edge of embarrassment. "I don't know...the same kind of dreams and wishes all adolescent girls have."

"Having never been an adolescent girl, I don't

have a frame of reference, so you'll have to be more specific," he teased.

She moved away from him, her laughter gone as a more sobering expression swept over her features. He could tell she was remembering those nights so long ago, when she'd sneak out of the house while her parents and sisters slept, to sit and dream in the moonlight. "I dreamed about love, about finding a special someone who would love me."

She smiled wistfully. "My sisters and I used to play pretend games beneath the dragon tree. Each of us wanted a prince to marry, but I never wanted one who might take me away from here. I wanted a prince who would help me build this ranch into the successful kind of place my dad always dreamed about." The smile fell away. "I thought I'd found him in Greg, but I was sadly mistaken."

Greg's name thrust Luke back to reality. And reality brought confusion. He thought of the tape-recorded message she'd played for him. She was right, the voice had been Greg's. The shock of hearing it had nearly undone Luke.

Not only had it shocked him, but it had also caused doubts to scurry around in his head...doubts about Abby's guilt. Somebody appeared to be playing games with her head. Why?

One thing was certain. Making love to Abby had been a mistake. He'd been a fool to think he could play the role of spy, get close to her and not get his emotions involved.

Now, with the scent of her still lingering on his

skin, with the honeyed taste of her still on his lips, his own deception tasted bitter.

He realized he couldn't carry out his plan any longer. He couldn't continue to deceive her about who he was and what he was really doing here.

He looked at her again. She smiled, the heartfelt smile of a sated woman. She looked beautiful with the sun shining on the golden strands of her hair and painting her skin in warm hues. As he remembered the velvet silkiness he'd experienced while loving her, he felt a stir deep in his groin.

Ignoring the reawakening desire, he sat up and reached for his jeans. He slid out of bed and stood. Somehow he felt it was better if he were dressed when he told her who he really was.

"Luke?"

He zipped up his pants, then looked at her, saw the curious frown that formed a wrinkle across her forehead. He raked a hand through his hair and sat on the edge of the bed. "Abby. We need to talk."

"You aren't going to confess that you're married, are you?" she asked, only half jesting.

"No, I'm not married." He stared at the wall, unable to look at her with her hair mussed from their lovemaking and her cheeks flushed with the residual color of pleasure.

"Luke?" She placed a hand on his arm and he heard the slight tremble of fear in her voice.

With effort, he turned to her. "Abby, my name isn't really Luke Black. It's Luke Foxwood. I'm Greg's half brother."

ABBY STARED AT HIM as if he'd spoken an unrecognizable language. He couldn't have said what she thought he had. "What...what did you say?"

"You heard me. I'm Greg's half brother."

The warmth and contentment that had flooded through her mere seconds before turned ice cold. She stared at him in confusion. "I don't understand. I didn't know Greg had any family. He never mentioned you."

She kept her anger, her hurt, at bay, wanting answers before she allowed her internal fury at his utter deception to overtake her. She reached for her robe, not wanting to be naked, feeling vulnerable now that she knew he'd lied to her about everything.

"Greg and I weren't very close." He got off the edge of the bed and moved to the window. Staring out, he continued. "I was eight years old when my dad left my mother and married Greg's mother. He was born soon after. We grew up in separate homes in different parts of the city. We didn't have a lot of contact until my father passed away. Greg was sixteen and I was twenty-four. Both our mothers had died before that and my father made me promise I'd take care of Greg."

He paused and drew a deep breath, his shoulders rigid with tension. "Greg ran away soon after moving in with me and I didn't hear from him again until about two months ago. He reappeared then and told me about his marriage to you and that he had a son."

Abby's head reeled with warring emotions, but the most prevalent was a feeling of betrayal, the hurt of finally trusting again and discovering herself a fool.

"Let me guess, he told you I was easy and good in bed so you thought you'd come out and give me a tumble." Her anger and bitterness rang in her tone.

He turned around and faced her once again. His dark eyes smoldered with emotion...emotions Abby couldn't begin to decipher. "No. He told me he'd put a lot of money into this ranch and when you divorced him he walked away with nothing. He told me that he continued to send you checks and yet you refused to allow him to see his son."

Abby snorted. "Your half brother was a liar...a trait that apparently runs in the family."

"He contacted me days before his murder and said he wanted to sue you for custody of Cody, wanted some form of legal remedy to regain all the money he'd given you before your divorce. I told him to let me come out here and check things out, see if something could be decided without a court battle. I thought I could work here a couple of days, find out what the situation was, perhaps talk you into being reasonable about allowing Greg access to Cody. Of course, before I could do much, Greg was murdered." He shifted uncomfortably and broke eye contact with her.

"And you believe I'm guilty of his death, and so this is your form of revenge?" She eyed him bitterly. "Congratulations, Luke. You've won the contest to see who is the biggest bastard in the Foxwood family."

He flinched. "Abby, I never meant for this to happen. I wanted to get close to you, find out if you were

responsible for Greg's death, but things went too
far.''

"Get out." Abby got out of bed and pulled her
robe tightly around her. "Pack your things and get
off my ranch."

"Abby..."

"Get the hell out of here, Luke." She felt as if
there were a band of steel around her chest, squeezing
her heart. She bit the inside of her cheek, forbidding
the tears that burned at her eyes from falling.

"Be reasonable." He took a step toward her and
she backed away, not wanting him to touch her.

Lies. He'd told her all lies. She'd trusted him, slept
with him, and he'd made love to her with the sole
purpose of gaining her trust to discover if she killed
his half brother. "I don't have to be reasonable. Don't
you remember? I'm a crazed killer. Now get out of
here before I call Bulldog to physically remove you."

"Abby, you're in lots of trouble. You need somebody on your side, somebody you can trust."

"Are you suggesting that somebody is you?" She
stared at him incredulously. She laughed, again bitterness rife in her voice. "After this you're the last
person I'd trust to be on my side. I didn't kill your
half brother. I had nothing to do with his death."

"Are you sure?"

For a moment his words hung in the air and sent a
shiver of apprehension up Abby's spine. She couldn't
pretend she didn't know what he was talking about.
He'd experienced one of her crazy mental blackouts
in person. She'd confessed to him that she had miss-

ing periods of time...time when she didn't know where she had been or what she had done.

But she knew...deep in her heart, in the core of her soul, that she couldn't have killed Greg. "You can ask me that after making love to me? You had doubts and still you slept with me? Just get out," she whispered in anguish.

He looked at her for another long moment, then did as she asked. He left the room and a moment later she heard the slam of the back door.

She sagged onto the bed...the bed that still retained his scent, his warmth. Damn him. The tears that had threatened earlier now flowed. Damn him for flirting with her, pretending to be attracted to her. Damn him for making her be attracted to him. Lies. All lies.

She stood and ripped the sheets off the bed. She'd wash them and hang them outside to dry, where the hot sunshine would banish any remainder of Luke's scent. She dropped the bedclothes by the bathroom door. First, a shower.

Beneath the hot spray of water, she thought of those moments of exquisite pleasure when Luke had claimed her so completely. She'd thought she'd felt his heart melding with her own, thought their love-making had been more than just a physical union. It had...it had been his manipulation.

Fool. She berated herself as she scrubbed her skin vigorously. How cruel Fate was to allow her to trust a man for the first time in years, only to have that man use her.

Damn him. And damn her own hide for wanting so desperately to believe in what she'd thought she'd seen in his eyes. Caring. Tenderness. And the heat of desire. That's what she'd thought she'd seen. She now realized any emotion she'd thought had radiated from his eyes had been coldly calculated and false.

Damn him. And damn her own weakness for wishing it weren't so...for wishing he really were Luke Black, a lonesome cowboy looking for love.

Chapter Ten

Luke slammed out of the house, angry that he'd told her the truth. He should have kept his mouth shut, should have continued his deception. He'd known that by telling her he'd make her angry. So why had he done it?

Because you needed the distance, a small voice answered inside him. He had gotten too close, and in those moments after making love to her, fear had resounded within him.

He walked toward the bunkhouse. What he needed most was a shower to wash away the memory of the feel of her in his arms.

Although she had demanded he pack his bags and leave the ranch, he intended doing no such thing. Something wasn't right here and he wasn't about to leave until he had some answers.

He owed it to Greg to find out who had killed him, and at this point Luke simply wasn't convinced beyond a doubt that it had been Abby. Even though he had witnessed her in some kind of a mental blackout the night before, even though he knew Greg had threatened to take Cody, he wasn't convinced that

Abby had killer instincts. And it would take killer instincts to bash a man in the head half a dozen times with a branding iron.

Then there was the question of those phone calls. Dammit, who was responsible for those? And why? Until he had more answers, there was absolutely no way he was leaving this ranch.

He walked into the bunkhouse and over to his locker. Spinning the combination wheel on the lock, he thought of the other men who shared this space with him. If Abby wasn't the killer, then it was quite possible one of these men might be responsible for Greg's death. But who...and why? What connection could Greg have had with any of these men?

He grabbed a shirt from his locker and pulled it on over his head, then sank onto the edge of his bed. He knew now that most of what Greg had told him had been lies.

Greg had always had a weak character and a fondness for easy money. Luke had hoped in his years on his own that Greg had changed his ways, matured to become a responsible, honorable man.

He thought of Cody's worn, well-read letters. Three letters from a man who had professed to Luke his desire, his eternal love, his need to see his son. It just didn't wash.

There had always been only one thing that motivated Greg, and that was greed. And if Luke had to guess, it wasn't his threats to pursue a relationship with his son that got him killed, it had been his voracious appetite for easy money.

He stood and decided to find Rusty. It had been

the old man who had initially hired him and, as far as he was concerned, Rusty would have to fire him. But Luke knew the ranch was understaffed and overworked. He had a feeling the foreman would be reluctant to see Luke go anytime soon.

Besides, he wanted to ask Rusty if he could borrow his truck to drive into town. It was time Luke reintroduced himself to Deputy Helstrom, let the officer know Luke's connection to Greg. He wanted to see the reports, the files from the investigation.

As he left the bunkhouse, from the corner of his eye he saw somebody slink around the edge of the barn. He frowned. For the past two days most of the men had been working in the pastures mending fences.

Curious, Luke followed his instincts and slid around the side of the barn. He saw a male figure running for the cover of the grove of trees behind the barn. "Hey!" he yelled.

The man hesitated a moment and turned to look at Luke, then continued to run away. Billy Sims. What was he doing here?

Luke didn't try to run after him, knowing Billy could easily lose him in the woods and had too big a lead on him. Instead he tried to figure out what the man had been doing. Had he been in the barn?

Luke thought of the nail that had wound up beneath Blackheart's saddle blanket. Billy had saddled the horse that day and Billy and Abby apparently had a history of trouble.

Luke walked into the dark coolness of the barn, the scent of horse, leather and hay welcoming him.

Blackheart nickered from his stall, apparently sensing his human presence. He went over to Blackheart, relieved to see the horse looked fine. Blackheart stretched his neck out in greeting and Luke petted his forehead. "I don't have any treats for you," Luke said to the animal as he stroked the dark hair.

Leaving the horse, Luke frowned once again, wondering what Billy Sims had been doing sneaking around the barn. On impulse he climbed the wooden stair to the loft and looked around. Bales of hay were stacked one on top of the other nearly to the ceiling, but nothing looked amiss.

He left the loft and leaned against the barn wall, eyeing the interior thoughtfully. Perhaps Billy hadn't been in the barn after all. In any case, it didn't look like he'd tried to do any damage.

Although most of the men working the ranch were affable and hard laborers, what bothered Luke was that each seemed to be more than a little secretive. Did one of them harbor the secret of murder?

Hearing footsteps outside the barn, Luke stepped into the darker shadows, wondering if Billy had returned.

Roger Eaton walked into the barn and directly to the workbench that stretched across the back wall. He grabbed a sackful of nails then turned around and gasped as Luke stepped out of the shadows. "Criminy, Luke, you scared the hell out of me." He gestured to the sack of nails he carried. "Rusty sent me back for these." Roger's lips turned up in a sly smile. "I noticed you didn't sleep in the bunkhouse last night.

I guess the boss lady has you doing personal work for her.''

Luke took a step toward the blond cowboy. "Be careful what you're insinuating."

The smile fell from Roger's lips. "Hey, no offense intended," he said quickly. "I just hope you're sleeping with one eye open," he added with a rueful shake of his head.

Luke eyed him curiously. "So you think Abby killed Greg?"

Roger shrugged. "I think it's more possible than not. From what I hear she had motive and opportunity. I figure if it walks like a duck and quacks like a duck…it's a duck."

"Isn't it possible it could be one of the ranch hands? They would have had access to the murder weapon and anyone could have snuck out of the bunkhouse on the night of the murder."

"Sure, I suppose that's possible," Roger agreed easily. "There's only one problem…why would any of the ranch hands want to kill Greg Foxwood? Personally, I never met the man and I imagine not many of the others had met him, either. Where's your motive?"

Motive. As Roger left the barn and hurried to deliver the nails Rusty had requested, Luke stared after him, his mind whirling. If Abby hadn't killed Greg, then somebody else had and there had to be a reason.

Motive. It was what tied Abby to the crime and was the missing link for any other suspect.

He left the barn and headed for the pasture, irritated by his thoughts, wondering why in the hell it was

suddenly so important to him that Abby be innocent
of the crime.

FOR THE REMAINDER of the morning Abby kept herself busy, trying to keep thoughts of Luke and his
betrayal at bay, but self-recriminations plagued her no
matter what she did.

After turning on the washer with the load of her
bedsheets, she went into the office to do a little paperwork. No matter how hard she tried to concentrate
on the numbers in the ledger, her mind rebelled and
instead formed visions of Luke.

She cursed herself for so easily allowing him to
crawl beneath her defenses. For six years she had kept
herself aloof, remained untrusting, and yet in the
space of a handful of days Luke had burrowed beneath her barriers and touched her in the most vulnerable emotional places.

After six years of being alone, she hadn't realized
how hungry she'd been not only for a masculine
touch, but for the company of a man, the gaze of an
interested male, all the things that make up a relationship.

She jumped as the phone rang, pulling her from her
thoughts. She stared at the instrument on the desk,
wondering if it would be another prank call, wishing
she had an answering machine. Taking a deep breath,
she snatched up the receiver, relieved to hear Bert
Manigan's voice.

"Tell me this isn't bad news," she said when he'd
identified himself.

"Darlin', prepare yourself. I wish it were good

news, but I spent the morning with the sheriff going over the files of your case, and in a bundle of canceled checks of yours he has five made out to Greg dated in the last ten days, totaling over two thousand dollars. Want to tell me what that's about?"

"I don't know what that's about. I didn't write any checks to Greg in the past ten days, let alone two thousand dollars' worth," Abby protested.

"Abby, honey, I've got copies of the checks right in front of me."

"I don't care what you have. I haven't written any checks to Greg in months and months."

"But you have written him checks in the past?" Bert asked.

Abby sighed. "Yes, I have. He'd call me crying hard times and hinting that if he had a little cash, he'd stay away from me and Cody. I know it was wrong, I know it was foolish, but over the years I occasionally sent him small amounts of money."

"This isn't good, Abby. The prosecution will attempt to use that information against you. They'll say Greg was extorting money from you and you grew tired of paying him."

"But that's not what happened and I haven't written a check to Greg in months," she said in frustration.

"Well, somebody wrote him checks on your account and signed your name." Bert read off the numbers of the checks and Abby wrote them down. When he hung up Abby had the feeling of a noose around her neck, a noose growing tighter and tighter.

She flipped to the back of the checkbook register

and found that the checks Bert had mentioned were missing. There were a total of ten missing checks, and they looked to have been hurriedly ripped out of the checkbook.

Who would have stolen the checks and made them out to Greg? Nothing made sense anymore. She slammed the checkbook closed and leaned her head against the cushioned backrest of the desk chair.

She'd always maintained an open door policy at the ranch, especially when it came to this office. At one time or another each and every one of her ranch hands had been either sent into this room to retrieve something or had come in here to be handed their paycheck. Any one of them would have had access and opportunity to steal the checks. But why would any one of them make those checks out to Greg?

It was impossible to imagine a stranger gaining access to the office. That left only one chilling possibility. Somebody Abby trusted—somebody close to her—had stolen the checks. Mystery built on mystery. Who'd killed Greg? Who'd paid him money? Who was making the phone calls to her? Her head felt ready to explode with all the frightening questions.

One thing was certain. She had not written those checks to Greg. She hadn't done it in her sleep, or in one of her strange blackouts. Both times she'd suffered one of her mental blackouts, she'd awakened knowing there was a missing chunk of time. Both times she'd immediately been aware of something wrong. Two times. That's all it had happened. She steadfastly ignored her uncertainty about the night of Greg's murder. Besides, she knew with certainty she'd never write two thousand dollars' worth of checks to Greg, not with the ranch finances as dismal as they were.

Two thousand dollars gone, money she'd assumed was in the account. She'd be lucky if they could meet payroll next week. She got up from the desk, too distracted by her thoughts to get any work done.

She looked at her wristwatch, surprised to realize it was after noon. Perhaps she'd eat a little lunch, then take a ride on Blackheart. She hadn't been on the horse since the day he'd thrown her and knew he'd be eager for a run.

In the kitchen, she stared at the refrigerator contents in dismay. If Maria didn't return from her sister's soon, they'd all starve unless somebody stepped into the position of cook.

She didn't know what they would do if Maria decided not to return to her job. Abby knew Maria's sister had health problems and there was a possibility that she would decide to remain with her sister to care for her.

Maria had worked for the family for as long as Abby could remember. *She would have had access to your closet,* a small voice whispered in the back of Abby's head. *She could have pulled the button off the blouse Deputy Helstrom confiscated.* Odd that her sister had gotten ill just as all hell had broken loose.

Abby shook her head in disgust. What was she thinking? How far had she sunk to believe that Maria, a trusted friend and part of her family, could possibly have any part in this mess?

She quickly made herself a sandwich, then sat at

the kitchen table, her head still reeling with suppositions.

Luke. Had he somehow gained access to her room? Snuck in while nobody else was in the house to rip the button from her blouse? Had he been making the phone calls to her, the ones that sounded like Greg? Was it all an attempt to make her break, cause her to confess her guilt?

Anger surged through her at thoughts of him. How quickly attraction could turn to hatred. And she did hate him. He'd lied to her, taken advantage of her weakness, her need for support and love. He'd pretended to care about her when in reality his sole purpose for being with her was to break her, force a confession from her.

She was still shocked that Greg had had a brother, even a half brother. He'd never talked about Luke, but then Greg had rarely spoken at all about his past. He'd told her once that he felt his life had truly begun on the day he'd met her. And in her youthful dreams of romantic love, she'd found his words thrilling and hadn't needed more than that.

She finished her sandwich and cleaned up her mess. Enough thoughts of Greg and Luke. Greg was dead and Luke was hopefully on a plane back to wherever he'd come from. They were both out of her life permanently.

What she needed was a good, fast ride on Black-heart to clear her head, chase away disturbed thoughts of Greg, and more intimate memories of Luke. Only this time, she intended to saddle the horse herself.

LUKE PULLED IN from his trip into town just in time to see Abby disappear into the barn. Apparently she was preoccupied because she didn't seem to notice Rusty's truck or Luke.

He parked and shut off the engine, frowning as he thought back over his conversation with Deputy Helstrom. Richard Helstrom had been shocked by Luke's announcement that he was Greg's half brother and had inquired at length about why Luke hadn't come forward the moment of Greg's death.

After several tense minutes of interrogation, Luke had taken control and demanded to see the investigation files and anything pertinent to the crime. He'd also demanded Greg's personal effects be released into his custody. Everything that had been on Greg's person the night of the murder now rested in a manila envelope on the seat next to Luke. Luke had also gotten permission to go into Greg's rented room and remove whatever belonged to Greg.

What he hoped was that in Greg's room there would be some clue as to whom Greg might have talked to, had dealings with before his murder. He hoped he'd find something the police had overlooked, some clue that would either definitively clear or inculpate Abby in the murder.

He also needed to tell her he had no intentions of leaving the ranch or returning to his home in Chicago until he was certain that justice would be met. He owed at least that much to Greg.

Gearing himself for the coming confrontation, he sucked in a deep breath, then got out of the truck. At the same moment Blackheart bolted out of the open door of the barn, his hooves stirring dust as he raced for the open pasture.

Luke stared after the riderless horse, then looked back at the barn door. Dread surged upward in his gut, tightening his throat with frantic anxiety. "Abby." Her name whispered from his lips, breaking the inertia that had momentarily gripped him.

He raced to the barn, his heart pounding painfully in his chest as the scent of danger encircled him. Inside, it took a moment for his eyes to adjust from the brilliant sunshine to the dim shadows.

Abby lay sprawled, unmoving, on the floor, a bale of hay next to her. "Abby!" This time her name wasn't a whisper, but rather exploded out of him as he raced to her side.

He crouched beside her, seeing the hay tangled in her hair and the position of the bale next to her. Apparently the bale had fallen and hit her. "Abby...Abby." He called her name and picked up her limp hand, but she remained still.

Had she been trying to carry a bale of hay and fallen down the stairs? Damn her and her independence. Gently, he felt her arms, her legs, seeking any broken bones, but he found none. Finally he eased her head off the ground and discovered a large lump on the back of her head. Probably the reason for her unconsciousness, he thought.

He scooped her up into his arms and carried her out of the barn and toward the house. She moaned slightly as he crossed the porch, but didn't open her eyes, didn't seem to be conscious.

Once inside, he placed her on the sofa, then went

into the bathroom and dampened a washcloth with cool water. He hurried back to her, his heart still beating a frantic rhythm. If she didn't come around pretty quickly, he'd need to call for a doctor.

The minute he placed the cool cloth across her forehead, her eyes fluttered, then opened. "Wh-what are you doing?" She began to sit up, then moaned and eased back down.

"Easy. You've been unconscious." Luke saw the fear that deepened the hue of her eyes. "No, not another blackout. I found you on the floor in the barn."

She frowned and he saw the fear fall away from her eyes. "Oh, yes. I was going to ride Blackheart. I saddled him, then I heard something...a noise. I thought somebody was in the barn. I walked out of the stall and...and that's all I remember."

"I think you must have been hit by a bale of hay falling from the loft."

"Yeah, well it feels like I got hit by a Mack truck." She sat up once again, this time without a moan, but with her hand at the back of her head. "What were you doing in the barn anyway? I thought I told you to pack your bags and leave."

"I've never done well at following directives. I borrowed Rusty's truck and went into town. When I pulled up, I saw you go into the barn, then a moment later Blackheart ran out. By the way, will he be all right? Last I saw him, he was heading for the pasture."

She nodded. "He'll come home on his own or one of the hands will bring him back."

Luke sank down next to her on the sofa, ignoring

her look of irritation. "If I were you, I wouldn't be in such a hurry to get rid of me."

"And why is that?"

The color coming back into her cheeks, along with the clarity in her eyes and the bite to her voice caused a wave of relief to flood through him. Apparently the bump on her head hadn't made her forget her anger with him. "Because I'm beginning to believe you aren't the one responsible for Greg's death."

She sighed impatiently. "That's what I've been saying all along."

"And, I think somebody threw that hay bale from the loft in an effort to intentionally harm you."

Abby stared at him as if he'd just lost his mind. She snatched the damp cloth from him and rubbed her forehead thoughtfully, then looked at him once again. "Why on earth would you think such a thing? The bale must have been stacked too close to the edge. It fell."

"I was up in the loft yesterday. There were no bales of hay anywhere near the edge of the loft. It's impossible that it was an accident."

Again an edge of fear darkened her eyes. "But why? Why would anyone want to hurt me?"

He shrugged. "Why is somebody calling you and pretending to be Greg? How did the nail get beneath Blackheart's saddle blanket the last time you rode?" He leaned closer to her, bringing with him the fresh, masculine scent she would forever identify as his. "Abby, something isn't right here and I'm beginning to think you're as much a victim as Greg was."

"Obviously something isn't right here. I've been

arrested for a crime I didn't commit and a dead man is calling me on the phone.'' His words caused a cold dread to grow inside her stomach, along with the dull throb in the back of her head. She realized he was merely stating aloud some of what she had been thinking and feeling.

She frowned, thinking back to those moments in the barn as she had finished saddling up Blackheart. She'd thought she'd heard the soft slap of footsteps, the rustle of movement. She'd left Blackheart's stall to see who'd come into the barn. She had a vague memory of somebody softly calling her name…then nothing. She looked at Luke in speculation. "So, exactly what do you have in mind?"

"Partners. We work together to find out who killed Greg, find out who's calling you, perhaps trying to harm you.''

She tried to stifle a snort of derision. "Partners? For all I know you're part of this craziness. You lied to me before. Why should I believe you're on my side in all this?"

His eyes were dark and enigmatic. "Because all I want is justice served. I want Greg's killer put behind bars.''

Despite her anger and hurt, despite the fact that she wanted to believe she hated him with every fiber of her being, hurt flickered through her at his words. Of course that was all he wanted. He wasn't staying at the ranch for any other reason, certainly not because of any feelings for her.

"Come on, Abby, work with me on this. We can start tomorrow morning. Richard Helstrom gave me the key to Greg's room. We can check it out to see if the police missed anything. If you aren't guilty, then help me find who is.''

Although she didn't want anything more to do with Luke, still ached at the depth of his betrayal in making love to her, she knew she couldn't figure all this out by herself. She needed him. As Greg's closest relative he'd know things about Greg, have access to information and the investigation she'd never gain alone. ''Okay, you can stay here and we'll see what we can find out about what's going on.''

''Partner?'' He held out his hand.

Abby hesitated a moment before she grasped his hand. ''Partner,'' she agreed, trying to ignore what his touch did to her.

He offered her a half smile. ''Don't look so worried. We're both after the same thing here.'' His gaze washed over her with languid heat, restirring embers of flames of desire in her.

She snatched her hand away, wondering if, indeed, they were after the same things. All she wanted was to somehow get through these traumas, get an opportunity to gain those long-ago, midnight wishes of her youth. Somehow she had the feeling that although Luke wanted to catch the real killer, he also intended to steal a piece of her soul in the process.

One thing was clear. By throwing in her allegiance with a man who'd already lied to her, betrayed her in the most base way, she exhibited the strongest evidence yet of being insane.

Chapter Eleven

"Hi, Luke. Mom said to tell you she'll be right out," Cody exclaimed as he met Luke at the truck the next morning. He grinned up at Luke, an open, toothless smile filled with sunshine. "I brought you something." The little boy dug into his pocket and withdrew a hickory nut. He held it out to Luke. "It's my good luck charm. See, I painted a face on it. I wanna give it to you."

Luke took the hard shell nut with the painted features making a happy face. "Why are you giving it to me?"

Cody smiled, a beatific expression that lit his entire face. "'Cause I like you." He immediately postured himself in like image to Luke, leaning against the truck and crossing his feet at the ankles.

"Thanks." As Luke pocketed the nut, an alien emotion fluttered in his chest, one that made him distinctly uncomfortable.

He didn't want to care about Cody, couldn't afford the emotional investment caring required. He'd tried to be a father figure once before in his life, with horrendous results. Although he'd enjoyed making love with Abby, he wasn't looking to fill the void his half brother left behind when he'd deserted her years ago. This was one of Greg's messes he simply couldn't clean up.

"Luke?"

"What?" Luke shifted positions, vaguely irritated when Cody did the same, once again mimicking his posture.

"You like my mom?"

Luke hesitated a moment, unsure how to answer, not wanting to feed any fantasies the little boy might entertain. "Sure, she's nice."

"And she's pretty, too. Huh?"

Luke was saved from answering by the slam of the front door and Abby's approach. As she walked toward the two males, Luke answered Cody's question in his mind. *Yes, she's pretty.* In fact, with the deep blue sundress clinging to her curves, and the sun sparkling on her hair, she looked more than pretty. And that set irritation winging through Luke once again.

"Sorry you had to wait," she said as she opened the driver's door of the truck and motioned Cody inside. "I'm dropping Cody at a friend's house in town."

"Yeah, I'm going to Jason's house. He's got a computer with lots of games," Cody said as he slid into the middle and Luke climbed in the passenger seat.

"And don't forget, we'll be back to pick you up around noon," Abby reminded him. She started the truck, not looking at Luke.

He remembered the warmth of her smile, the easy,

flirtatious relationship they'd shared before he'd told her his true identity. A small arrow of regret pierced through him. There would be no warmth or flirtation today. It was obvious she considered him and his presence a necessary evil. So be it.

He stared out the window at the passing scenery, trying to ignore Cody's chatter as the little boy filled up the silence that stretched between the two adults. He didn't want to be sucked any deeper into Cody's need for a father or Abby's desire for a soul mate. All he wanted was to find a killer, then get back to his own life in Chicago.

"Don't ya think, Luke?"

Cody's voice pulled him from his inward thoughts. "What? I'm sorry, I didn't hear you."

"Don't ya think we should have a party at the ranch on the Fourth of July?"

"Cody, I'm sure Luke won't be at the ranch by then," Abby answered.

Cody turned bright blue eyes on Luke. "Where will you be? Why won't you be here?"

"I'll be in Chicago," Luke answered. "That's where I live."

Cody stared at him in disbelief, then shook his head in confusion. "That's silly. You're a cowboy and cowboys don't live in Chicago."

"Maybe I'm just one of those pretend cowboys you told me about," Luke replied.

Again Cody looked at him, studying him with concentration. "Nope, you're a real cowboy. I wouldn't give my good luck hickory nut to a pretend cowboy."

Luke noticed the way Abby's lips were tightly

compressed, as if she were having difficulty biting back choice comments. He was surprised to realize he appreciated her reticence. Although he had no intention of being a part of Cody's life, oddly enough he didn't want the young boy thinking badly of him.

Minutes later they pulled up in front of Cody's friend's home. "Tell MaryAnn I said thanks and we'll be back to get you around noon," Abby reminded her son as he ran toward the front door of the attractive ranch house.

"Okay," he agreed. He was met at the door by a tall brunette who waved to Abby as Cody raced through her front door.

"I won't have him hurt," Abby said softly as she pulled away from the curb.

"You've obviously worked me into some sort of monster in your mind if you think I would consciously hurt a little kid," Luke observed dryly.

"I just want you to be conscious of the fact that for some incomprehensible reason Cody thinks you're great. The fact that he gave you his hickory nut means he's chosen you as a special person in his life."

"There was a time not so long ago that I had the feeling you thought I was rather great." He wasn't sure why he was baiting her. Perhaps to shatter her aloofness. He would prefer anger to the cool indifference she'd shown him since they'd gotten into the truck.

"That was before I discovered you were a liar. And as far as I'm concerned liars are right down there with crooks and swindlers."

A stain of color flushed her cheeks and Luke felt

a flash of desire hit him in the midsection as he remembered the heat of her kisses, the satin softness of her skin. "The next time we make love I'll remind you of my real name before, during and after."

If not for his seat belt, his head would have crashed through the front window as she jammed on the brakes and squealed to a stop. She turned in her seat and faced him, her eyes flashing anger. "Trust me on this, Luke. I don't intend for there to be a next time. I've had both the Foxwood men and I've found them both lacking in one very important area."

"I've never had any complaints before," he protested.

She rolled her eyes in exasperation. "Oh, stop being so...so...male. I'm not taking about your prowess. I'm talking about the fact that you lack honor."

"I did a dishonorable thing, but I'm not a dishonorable man," Luke countered.

She sighed in obvious aggravation, then jumped as a car behind them honked. "You're holding up traffic," Luke said.

She slammed the truck into gear and took off once again. "All I know is I've had it with Foxwood men, and I'll never, ever sleep with you again."

"Ah, you tempt Fate when you make absolutes. Hasn't anyone ever told you before never to say never?"

"Never say never unless you mean it, and I mean it," she replied.

Luke smiled, amused by her vehemence. Intellectually, he was certain she meant what she said, but she couldn't hide the pulse pounding in the hollow of her neck, or the desire that masked itself within her anger.

He had a feeling she wanted him again, and that suited him just fine because he wanted her, too. He leaned back in the seat and smiled to himself. Before he left the ranch to return to Chicago he intended to have Abby one last time.

HIS SMILE IRKED Abby to distraction, just as his familiar scent had from the moment he'd climbed into the truck. Damn him for making her remember the pleasure of lovemaking, the sweet surrender that made the world stop spinning and time stand still. Damn him for bringing back the memory of what it felt like to be in love.

Of course she wasn't in love with Luke, but still in those moments when he'd held her so close, whispered her name in a lover language, she'd given him a piece of herself she knew she'd never get back.

She shoved these thoughts aside, needing to focus on their business, the reason why they were together right now. "Where did you say Greg's room was?"

He pulled a sheet of paper from his pocket. "The Sandford Motel. Know where it is?"

She nodded. "It's not really a motel anymore. Gus Sandford owns it and a couple of years ago started renting out the rooms by the week or month rather than just overnight."

"Deputy Helstrom said Greg was here nearly three weeks before his death."

Abby shot Luke a look of surprise. "I didn't realize he'd been in town that long. Somebody told me he was back about ten days before he and I met up in the diner.''

"What we need to do is try to recreate what Greg did in those three weeks. We need to find out who he had contact with, what he got himself mixed up in.''

"Won't the police have all that information?" Abby asked.

"The police don't care. They believe they've arrested the guilty person.''

"Me.'' Overwhelming despair blew through Abby like the cold winds of winter sweeping down the mountainsides. "We've got to find something, some clue to clear my name. My trial is in five weeks.''

"Whatever leads or clues we find, we'll follow and see where they take us.''

She shot him a speculative glance. "Do you believe I'm innocent?" Immediately she wished she could recall the question, knowing she shouldn't give a damn what he thought.

He paused for a long moment. "I don't know, Abby," he finally said. "I do know this, there are too many questions unanswered, too many things happening that make no sense. I also believe there was a rush to judgment because Richard Helstrom has a vested interest in seeing you put away, and that bothers me.''

Abby nodded. At least he wasn't lying and pretending to believe in her innocence without reservation.

She pulled into the parking lot of the old motel where Greg had been living before his death. From the exterior, the place looked like the last bus stop before hell.

The colorful neon sign that had once blinked a cheerful welcome now hung broken and the rosy paint had dulled and peeled with age and neglect.

"Not exactly the Ritz, huh?" Luke observed as they got out of the truck.

"But it's cheap and I imagine Greg didn't plan on spending the rest of his life here."

"He was in unit five. Deputy Helstrom gave me the key."

It took them only a few minutes to locate unit five around the back of the low, long building. As Luke opened the door, dank stale air hit them in the face. Dark curtains were drawn closed across the windows and Luke immediately strode to them and opened both the curtains and windows, allowing in the bright sunshine and fresh air.

However, even the sunshine couldn't banish the overall air of utter misery and despair that filled the room. An old gold bedspread covered the bed and the nightstand was scarred with glass rings and cigarette burns. Take-out food containers littered the small table, their rancid scent lingering in the air.

Abby wondered if the food containers were Greg's, or if the police had sat at the table and eaten during their search of the room.

"What a dump," Luke said, surveying the room with a touch of sadness in his eyes.

Abby thought she knew what he was thinking. How sad that a place like this would be a man's last stop. How sad that at the end of Greg's life, all he'd left behind was a suitcase full of clothes in a cheap rented room.

As she tried to imagine what she'd feel like if it were one of her sisters that had brought them here, she felt a small surge of sympathy for Luke. It would be difficult for any family member to see this room, the utter hopelessness that it contained.

"It's sad, isn't it?" she finally said softly.

Luke nodded. "Yeah, it is. When Greg was younger, I constantly hounded him about his life choices, about setting goals and achieving some measure of success. In the years after he ran away, I hoped that's what he'd done." He raked a hand through his hair, stress lines radiating from the corners of his eyes and around his mouth. "Let's get to it. Why don't you go through the dresser drawers, and I'll check out the suitcase."

They worked in silence, going through clothing, looking under furniture, in dark corners, anywhere there might be anything that would be a clue to whom Greg might have been in contact with in the weeks before his death.

"This is hopeless," Abby said nearly two hours later as she finished looking through the contents of the medicine cabinet in the bathroom. "If there was anything here that might help, the police must have picked it up." She left the bathroom and sat on the edge of the bed as Luke turned and stared out the window.

What little they had found was in the center of the bed. Scraps of paper with names or numbers, matchbook covers all from the same local bar and an envelope of money Luke had found taped to the frame beneath the bed. "I wonder how the police missed all this," Abby said.

Luke turned from the window and looked at her. "Apparently they didn't dig too deep, but did just a cursory search." He joined her on the bed and stared at the pile of miscellaneous items. "However, I do find it interesting that this envelope contains over three thousand dollars in cash. Where would Greg have gotten it and why hide it?"

"According to what Bert Manigan told me, two thousand of it came from my bank account." She quickly filled him in on what Bert had told her about the checks made out to Greg from her.

"And you don't remember writing them?"

"More than that, I'm positive I didn't write them. The only thing I can figure out is that somebody stole the checks from the office and forged my signature on them. Why that somebody made them out to Greg is anyone's guess."

"But that tells us something we'd already suspected," Luke said. "That Greg was in contact with somebody at the ranch."

"But who?" Again despair swept through Abby. "I've got a dozen men working for me at the ranch and as you know Rusty doesn't exactly do background checks on them before he hires them. I don't know much more about them than their names, and in some cases that's not even the truth," she finished with a pointed glare.

He raised his hands defensively. "Let's not get into that again." He picked up the envelope of cash and held it out to her. "You might as well take this. From what you've said, it probably came from your account."

"Shouldn't we turn it in to the police?" Abby asked.

Luke shrugged. "Why? They didn't find it. The cash doesn't yield any clues to the murder, and all it will do if we turn the envelope over to them is tie up the money where nobody can use it. Go ahead, take it. Apply it toward your defense fund."

Abby took the envelope, then watched as Luke picked through the other items on the bed. He grabbed one of the half dozen matchbook covers. "These are all from the same place," he observed.

Abby nodded. "The Wild Coyote Bar. It's a little dive on the edge of town."

"In order to have all these matchbooks, Greg probably had to spend some time in the bar."

A flare of excitement shot through her as she thought of something. "Lots of the men at the ranch hang out there in their spare time. If Greg was working with somebody at the ranch, the odds are good they met in the bar."

"Then we need to go to the bar." Luke stood.

Abby also rose from the bed. "We can't go now. It's almost time to get Cody. Besides, I'm sure it's not even open until night."

"Then we'll go tonight."

Abby frowned thoughtfully. "From what I've heard, it's a pretty rough place. Junior has always said he wished it would burn down and save him the usual nightly fights and drunken disturbance calls."

"If you don't feel comfortable going, then stay at home. I'll go by myself and see what I can learn."

Abby eyed him in speculation. "No, I'll go. I want to be there when we get answers. I don't want to depend on your spin on what you hear. It's my life on the line here."

"Don't you trust me?" he asked, a small smile playing at the corners of his mouth. The smile was devastating and, coupled with a wicked shine in his eyes, caused a sensual heat to unfurl in the pit of her stomach.

"No, I don't." She broke their eye contact and reached for her purse. When she looked at him, the smile had faded and instead he gazed at her with the same kind of speculation she'd given him moments before.

"Maybe that makes us even, because I'm not sure I trust you, either. Come on, let's get out of here."

He left the room and Abby followed after him, amazed by his last words and disconcerted by the realization that she wasn't sure deep down that she trusted herself to be innocent in Greg's death.

Chapter Twelve

The Wild Coyote Bar lived up to its name. Built in the middle of a grove of trees on the outskirts of town, the wooden building looked as if it had been through several wars.

Although it was only a few minutes after eight o'clock, already the place pulsed with the rhythm of too many drunks and too loud music. The parking lot was packed and it took Abby several minutes to finally find an empty space.

"I hope this isn't a mistake," she finally said once they were parked. "This is the kind of place my mother always warned me to stay away from."

"Worried about your reputation?" Luke smiled.

Abby laughed nervously. "Funny, isn't it? Everyone thinks I'm a murderer, but I don't want anyone to think I hang out in disreputable places. Maybe I really am nuts." She stared at the bar, reluctant to get out of the truck and go inside. "I decided I'm going to call my doctor, make an appointment to see if he can figure out what's going on with my blackouts." She looked at Luke. "I'm terrified of what he might find."

To her surprise Luke leaned over and took her hand. For a moment she allowed the heat and strength of his grasp to comfort her, ease her fears. "It's important you find out what's happening with you. We need to know if you suffered a blackout the night that Greg was killed."

Abby snatched her hand away, reminded once again of the reason Luke was here, what his ultimate goal was in being with her. "We may never know for sure whether I suffered a blackout that night, but I know I didn't kill Greg. I'm not capable of that kind of violence." And she resented the fact that Luke had held her in his arms, made sweet love to her, and didn't realize it was impossible for her to commit murder.

She opened her door, irritated by how easily he could affect her with just a simple touch. "Let's get this over with," she said as she got out of the truck.

Despite her irritation with Luke, she was grateful for his presence next to her as they entered the bar. The interior was dim, with a thick layer of smoke that lay like a veil across the low ceiling. The jukebox in one corner blared the latest Alan Jackson hit and several couples danced in drunken movements on the small sawdust-covered dance floor.

"Hey, little lady, ain't never seen you in here before." A cowboy leaned toward Abby with a smile, nearly falling off his bar stool in the process.

"And you'll never see me in here again," Abby replied as she took a step closer to Luke.

"Come on, let's talk to the bartender." Luke placed an arm around her shoulder, glared at the drunk on the stool, then led her to the other end of the long wooden bar where the bartender was talking to a young woman.

"What can I get for you?" he asked as Luke and Abby slid onto stools.

"Two beers," Luke said. "And perhaps a little information."

The bartender looked like a man who had once been a prizefighter. His nose was flat and scar tissue formed a knot across one eyebrow. The glare he shot at Luke didn't improve his forbidding countenance. "I'll get you two beers, but I'm not no information booth."

"What kind of information are you looking for, handsome?" the woman next to Luke asked as the bartender turned to get their drinks.

Luke turned around on the stool and offered her a sexy smile. The woman's heavily lined eyes flared with a spark of feminine interest and Abby had the ridiculous impulse to hit both of them upside their heads.

"You a regular in here?" Luke asked.

The bartender snorted. "If Dotty here gets any more regular she's gonna start having to help pay the taxes on this place." He slammed two full beer mugs down in front of them. "You two the heat?" he asked, his gaze suspicious.

"No, we aren't cops," Luke replied. "We don't care whether your liquor license is current or if you serve minors."

"Huh, a minor bellies up to my bar, I kick his

butt," the bartender exclaimed. "So, if you aren't cops, what kind of information are you looking for?"

"You know any of the workers from the Connor spread?" Luke asked.

"I do," Dotty said, and smiled coyly as Luke looked at her once again. "I've danced with them, drank with them. One of them, the blond named Roger, tried to pick me up one time by telling me he was a son of some congressman." She laughed and shook her head. "I thought I'd heard every line a man could throw at a woman, but that was definitely a new one."

"Who else have you seen in here from the Connor place?"

Dotty shrugged. "I figure all the men have been in at one time or another. The old man, Rusty, comes in occasionally and Billy is in here almost every night." She frowned. "Although he's definitely not the friendly sort. He usually sits in the corner and drinks until he's nearly passed out."

"Did you know a man named Greg Foxwood?" Abby asked, wanting to cut to the chase and get out of the bar.

Dotty leaned forward, her eyes widened. "You mean the guy who was murdered, right?" Abby nodded and Dotty continued. "Yeah, I knew him." She shivered and wrapped her arms around her shoulders. "What a trip, one week I'm rolling around in his bed, and the next week he's dead."

Abby flushed. She didn't want to know intimate details about what Greg had done with various women in the weeks before his murder. "Did you ever see Greg talking to any of the men from the Connor ranch?''

Dotty's eyes narrowed. ''You're his ex-wife, aren't you? The one they've arrested for his murder?'' Dotty grinned. ''I don't blame you, honey. He was a fine-looking man, but it was easy to see he had the wanderlust. Hell, I wasn't the only woman in here he slept with.''

Abby took a sip of her beer, appalled that Dotty had given her approval for supposedly killing Greg. Abby was out of her realm of reality. Resentment toward Greg flooded through her. She resented him for sucking her down into such an ugly piece of the world.

''So, did you see Greg having conversations with any of the men from the Connor ranch?'' Luke picked up the questioning where Abby had left off.

Dotty frowned thoughtfully. ''I don't remember anything specific, but this is a small place and Greg was a friendly man. I'm sure he probably talked to all of them.''

Abby touched Luke's arm. ''Let's get out of here. This is a dead end.''

Luke nodded and took a couple deep drinks of his beer. Then, throwing a few dollars on the bar, he stood. ''Thanks for your time and your help,'' he said to both the bartender and Dotty. The bartender grunted and Dotty smiled.

''Anytime, handsome,'' she replied, casting him another smile that indicated she'd love more time with him if he'd lose Abby's company.

Abby and Luke had just about reached the door

when it opened and Billy Sims walked in. His dark eyes widened in shock as he saw them. Immediately he turned and began to make his way to a table in the corner. Before he could get there, Luke grabbed his arm.

"I want to talk to you, Sims," he said.

Abby was as surprised as Billy at Luke's demand. "About what?" Billy asked with a dash of belligerence.

"About what you were doing in Abby's barn yesterday."

"I don't have to talk to you about nothing," Billy exclaimed. He tried, unsuccessfully, to tear his arm from Luke's grasp.

"I think you do—that is, unless you want to be implicated in a charge of attempted murder."

Abby wasn't sure who gasped louder, her or Billy. "What are you talking about?" This time Billy managed to jerk out of Luke's grasp, but he made no attempt to move away from them.

"I'm talking about the fact that somebody tried to kill Abby by throwing a bale of hay from the loft yesterday and I saw you in the barn before it happened."

Abby looked at Luke sharply, wondering why he hadn't mentioned seeing Billy in the barn before now. They'd been partners for less than twenty-four hours and already he was withholding information from her.

"You're crazy," Billy replied. "I wouldn't do anything like that. I wouldn't try to hurt Miss Connor."

"Then what were you doing in the barn?"

"I had to get something." Billy stared down at his

feet, refusing to meet either of their gazes. "Something that I'd forgotten."

"What, Billy? What did you take?"

Abby felt pressure build in her chest as she waited for his answer. Why had he been in her barn after she'd fired him? Had he stolen a branding iron? Had he intended to implicate her in yet another crime?

"I had a stash hidden in the barn," Billy mumbled, his words barely audible.

"A stash? I don't understand," Abby said.

"Booze," Luke answered flatly. "Is that right?"

Billy nodded. "I had a couple bottles hidden in the barn. Yesterday I went back to get them." For the first time he looked directly at Abby. "But I swear, I didn't throw no hay bale at you. I was mad 'cause you fired me, but I'd never try to hurt nobody."

Abby believed him. She'd had her share of mean men working at the ranch. But Billy, although not particularly well liked by the other workers, had not had a reputation as a brawler or a vicious man. Rather he'd been viewed with a combination of disgust and pity.

"Come on, Luke. Let's go home," she said, suddenly exhausted. The day had begun with such promise. She'd been sure that by thoroughly checking Greg's room they would find proof in some shape or form of her innocence.

Even on the way to the bar, she'd retained the hope that somehow they'd find some answers, that somebody in the bar held the secrets she needed to be cleared.

As she and Luke walked back to the truck, her

despair lay heavy in her heart. What if they never found anything to absolve her? The thought caused her to stumble. She pitched forward, gasping as Luke grabbed her and steadied her close against him.

"You all right?" His breath was warm against her temple.

She nodded, fighting the need to lean against him, to allow him to wrap her in his arms and keep her safe. But she knew that wasn't what he offered her. He was here to find a killer and for no other reason.

"I'm fine," she said as she stepped back from him. "Discouraged, but fine."

"You shouldn't be discouraged," Luke said once they were in the truck and heading back to the ranch. "We now know there is a definite possibility of a connection between somebody at the ranch and Greg."

"Yeah, but a connection with whom? This doesn't help me at all."

"Sure it does," Luke countered. "At least your lawyer can make a reasonable alternative theory for Greg's murder, that he fought with somebody from the ranch who later took a branding iron and used it to kill him."

"I don't want alternative theories, I want to be able to go into court with positive proof that I'm innocent." To her horror, her last words ended on a sob. She gulped, swallowing convulsively as she fought for control, but the tears came faster and faster. She couldn't wipe them away fast enough to keep them from blurring her vision.

"Pull over. I'll drive." Luke's voice was filled

with a touch of sympathy and Abby didn't hesitate to take him up on the offer.

She swerved over onto the shoulder and stumbled from the truck, sobs still pressing thickly against her chest. Despair overwhelmed her, deeper, more profound than any she'd ever experienced in her life. She had no defenses left, no strength to still the tears.

Luke met her at the front of the truck and rather than passing her to get into the driver's seat, he pulled her against him, holding her tight as she continued to cry.

Despite her desire not to, Abby gave in to her need to cling to him. The darkness of the night, and the isolation of the area where she'd pulled over helped by giving her a sense of privacy.

She cried until there were no more tears left, only gasping dry hiccups that she found enormously embarrassing. She finally disentangled herself from him. "Thanks," she murmured, averting her face from his view.

His palms cupped each side of her face, forcing her to look up at him. "Abby, there's no shame in needing a shoulder to cry on. There's no disgrace in not being strong all the time."

Abby stiffened and pushed away from him. "I know," she said softly, then went around the truck and got into the passenger seat.

Easy for him to say, she thought as he started the truck. Certainly there was no shame in needing somebody to comfort you, hold you up when the world's weight got too heavy. That's what people who cared about each other did. But she'd be a fool to depend

on Luke Foxwood. He didn't care about her and she
resented the fact that he pretended he did. More than
that, she resented the fact that she wanted him to care.

LUKE FELT Abby's frustration as it filled the interior
of the truck cab. In truth, the same emotion rolled
around inside him. He felt his shirt, the dampness
from her tears still evident. Her tears had touched
him, more than he'd thought possible. Since his time
at the ranch he'd come to admire her strength, and
her uncharacteristic tears had shaken him.

"Abby, I know you're disappointed. I was hoping
to get some answers, too." He finally broke the silence as they pulled up in front of the house. He shut
off the engine, then turned to face her. "All this
means is that we need to dig deeper, question more
people."

"It's hopeless," she said, her voice flat and tone-
less. "I'll go to prison and either Richard Helstrom
or Henry Carsworth will end up owning the ranch."
She stared blankly out the front window. "Hank and
Colette will be all right. They have each other and
Hank can find work anywhere. But Belinda will be
all alone...and Cody..." She pressed her lips tightly
together, as if thoughts of her son threatened to undo
her temporary hold on her composure.

"You never struck me before as a quitter," Luke
replied. "But if you're ready to roll over and play
dead, then I guess you deserve to lose the ranch and
your freedom."

He got the response he wanted. Her back stiffened
and her eyes flashed with fire as she jerked back to

look at him. "That's easy for you to say," she snapped. "No matter what happens when this is all over, you'll just get on your horse and ride away, back to your own life in Chicago. Meanwhile I've got five weeks to figure out who committed a horrid crime and no clues to follow. I'm not about to give up, but I'm allowed to be momentarily discouraged."

Luke grinned and nodded. "Good, that's better."

She studied his features for a moment, then returned his smile. "You did that on purpose."

"Anger is always better than despair." He handed her the keys to the truck. "I wouldn't turn down a cup of coffee if someone was to invite me in for one."

She nodded. "Okay. I think I could use a cup of hot cocoa myself."

They got out of the truck and went into the house. "Go on in and have a seat." Abby motioned toward the kitchen. "I'll just be a minute, I want to check on Cody."

As she disappeared down the hall, Luke went into the kitchen. He found the coffee and started a pot, trying not to remember that the last time he'd made coffee in this kitchen it had been before a sweet session of lovemaking with Abby.

He tried not to think of that, knew such thoughts would only increase his own frustration. And he was frustrated. He no longer knew what to believe, no longer knew why he remained here in Cheyenne. He should return to Chicago, let the judicial system and the legal authorities figure out who killed Greg and who should be punished.

He sank down at the table, his thoughts moving from Abby to Greg. Seeing that horrible room where Greg had lived the last of his days had been difficult. Profound sadness had arrowed through him, a sadness coupled with enormous guilt.

"Thanks for starting the coffee," Abby said as she walked into the kitchen.

He nodded. "Cody all right?"

"Sound asleep and Belinda is reading." She got a cup from the cabinet and heated water in the microwave. "I worry about her, she spends too much time alone. Sometimes I think Belinda prefers the animals on the ranch to people."

"At least with animals you always know where you stand. They aren't capable of deceit or manipulation." He sighed and watched for a moment as Abby opened a container and added a tablespoonful of what appeared to be cocoa mix to her hot water. "While I was waiting for you, I was thinking about Greg, and all his deceit and manipulations over the years."

Abby poured and set her cup on the table, then poured his coffee and joined him. "Greg wasn't really a wicked man, he was just weak, always looking for fast money, the easy way out of any problem."

Luke frowned and wrapped his hands around the warm cup in front of him. "Yeah, but I keep thinking maybe if I'd done something different when he came to live with me he would have turned out differently."

"What would you have done differently?" Abby took a drink of her chocolate, her gaze curious.

"Been more stern, been less stern, I don't know." He sighed. "I just feel like I might have made a difference in Greg's life if only I'd tried harder."

"That kind of thinking is crazy." Abby leaned back in her chair and took another sip of her drink. "It's exactly the way I felt for months after Greg left me." Her eyes darkened with her memories. "I thought if only I'd been more understanding, a better wife. If only I'd done something different, he would have stayed."

"You must have loved him a lot."

She smiled, a sad little gesture that touched Luke's heart as strongly as her tears had before. "I thought I loved him, but I realize now what I thought was love was more of an infatuation and a need to have somebody by my side. My parents had just died and Greg seemed so strong, so sure of himself." She shrugged. "We were both very young."

"But you grew up and I don't think Greg did."

"I had to grow up. I had a baby to take care of, two younger sisters looking to me for leadership and a ranch to run." She finished her hot chocolate, then looked at him blankly. "What were we talking about?"

"Greg." Luke noticed the hazy unfocus in her eyes and he leaned toward her. "Abby, you feeling all right?"

"I feel fine. In fact, I feel wonderful." She didn't look at him, but rather seemed fascinated by the wall behind his head. "Everything looks so bright, so vivid. Can you see the colors, Luke?"

Adrenaline flooded Luke as he realized something

had happened to her. Somewhere in the space of the past ten minutes or so, she'd drifted into a muddled mental state. Her eyes held the same foggy, dreamlike quality they'd had on the night he'd found her up in the dragon tree.

"Abby, maybe you should go to bed now?" he suggested, his mind whirling as he tried to figure out what had set her off, what possibly might have caused her to lose touch with reality.

"No, I don't want to go to bed." She stood, stumbling slightly. "I want to ride Blackheart and feel the night wind on my face." She closed her eyes, a smile curving her lips as if she already felt the caress of a night wind. "Yes...yes, I'll go for a ride." She opened her eyes and started for the door, then gasped in surprise as Luke grabbed her arm and stopped her forward progress.

"Abby, a ride on Blackheart isn't a good idea," he said.

"It's not?" A small wrinkle appeared between her brows. "But why?"

"It's late. Blackheart is probably sleeping. You don't want to disturb his rest this late at night." Luke knew he was babbling and as he continued listing reasons she shouldn't go riding, she reached up her hands and placed them on either side of his face.

She stared at his face with an unnatural concentration and intensity. Her fingers didn't remain still, but rather danced over the surface of his skin, as if she were blind and she was reading his features through her fingertips.

Despite the bizarreness of the situation, her touch

evoked a surge of desire within him. The sweet scent of her perfume reminded him of the honeyed taste of her kisses, the evocative sounds she'd made when he'd made love to her.

But desire fought with concern and a curiosity of what had happened to make the change in her. She'd been fine before she'd started drinking her cup of hot chocolate. Any flicker of desire fled his mind at this thought.

He stepped away from her and grabbed the tin of the dry mix he'd watched her add to the hot water. "Abby, who else drinks this stuff?" he asked.

"Me. Only me."

"Cody doesn't drink it...or either of your sisters?"

She shook her head, the wrinkle once again back in her forehead. "They don't like it. Just me. I'm the only one who likes to drink it."

Luke opened the lid and stared into the dark, powdery mixture. "Abby, the night you climbed into the dragon tree, did you have a cup of cocoa before then?"

"Oh, Luke, the dragon tree." Her eyes gleamed with excitement. "Let's go find the dragon tree."

He realized he wasn't going to get rational answers from her tonight. She was in a world of her own, and the best he could do was make sure she stayed safe and unharmed.

He stared down thoughtfully at the cocoa mix, his mind whirling with suppositions. Was it possible Abby was being drugged? It seemed odd that she'd been fine, rational, before taking the drink. Had she been drugged the night of Greg's death? And if what he thought was true, then who was responsible? "Abby, where do you get this stuff?"

He looked up and his blood ran cold. The back door stood open and Abby was gone.

Chapter Thirteen

"Abby." Luke called into the darkness of the night. He narrowed his eyes, trying to see her form in the sliver of moonlight that peeked out from behind a bank of clouds. Dammit, how could she have disappeared so quickly? She was in no condition to run wild in the dark.

He headed for the dragon tree, instinctively knowing that's where he'd probably find her. As he ran, his mind whirled. If Abby was being drugged, was it by the same person who called and pretended to be Greg? And if so, for what reason?

Motive. Everywhere he turned that's what seemed to be missing. If somebody else had killed Greg, then what was the motive? If somebody was drugging Abby, then what was the motive? He knew the two had to be tied together by threads of evil. As far as the phone calls went, the voice Luke had heard on the tape recorder had been Greg's voice, not somebody mimicking it. But how in the hell was that possible?

All suppositions and possibilities fled his mind as he reached the dragon tree and found Abby huddled at the base. She looked like a frightened child, with her knees drawn up to her chest and her hands covering her eyes.

"Abby?" He called her name softly.

"Luke. I'm so scared. Something is wrong with me. Something is so wrong. Everything is too bright, my eyes hurt, my brain hurts." She didn't remove her hands from her face and Luke's heart ached for her helplessness.

"Abby, let me take you back inside. You need to sleep. When you wake up, everything will be fine."

"You promise?"

"I promise," Luke said. Before she could resist him, before her mind could whirl in yet another direction, he leaned down and scooped her up into his arms.

She turned into his chest and wrapped her arms around his neck, clinging with trust while keeping her eyes tightly closed.

As Luke carried her toward the house, a slow, burning rage filled his chest. Who was responsible for this? Who had turned a strong, vibrant, independent woman into a clinging, helpless shell of herself? Who was playing mind games with her? Making phone calls from beyond the grave, stealing checks and paying them to Greg?

He took her right to her bedroom and placed her on the bed. As she remained stiff, with eyes closed, he gently removed her shoes and socks. When he'd finished, she opened her eyes and stared at him, her fear changing the blueness of her eyes to near black.

"What's happening to me? What's wrong with me?" she whispered.

"Shh, we'll talk about it in the morning." He pulled down the blankets and urged her under, then sat in the chair next to the bed. He leaned over and stroked her forehead. "How are you feeling?"

"Dizzy...the walls are breathing. I can see them moving in and out." She closed her eyes once again. "It's better with my eyes closed...like looking in a kaleidoscope." She sighed. "Don't stop," she murmured as he paused in his caress of her forehead.

"I won't. I'll be right here for as long as you want me." He remained at her side long after she'd fallen asleep. It wasn't just fear that she'd awaken and do something crazy that kept him next to her, but something deeper.

During their lovemaking Luke had felt a connection forged, a bond that went deeper than their flesh. And in each day since he'd felt that connection growing stronger. It went beyond admiration into an emotional caring he'd never experienced before. He didn't want to analyze it, didn't even want to contemplate that it might have a future. He knew better. He had no place in Abby's life, wasn't the kind of "real" cowboy Cody wanted as a father. He was simply a grieving half brother to a man whose death had left behind a mess. Once the mess was cleaned up, he'd be gone.

ABBY AWOKE SLOWLY, lingering in the twilight state between the unconsciousness of deep sleep and the consciousness of full awakening. Warmth surrounded her, the masculine warmth of an embrace. It felt good. She didn't question it, wondered only if she were immersed in a particularly vivid dream.

"Hey, Mom, what's Luke doing in your bed?" Cody's voice ushered in a cold blast of reality.

Abby's eyes snapped open at the same time Cody bounded onto the bed and Luke sat up. "Does this mean you really are gonna be my stepdad? Huh, Luke? Is that why you're in my mom's bed?"

Luke jumped off the bed as if he'd been shot out of a cannon. Abby stared at him blankly, then as vague memories from the night before flurried through her head, she turned her attention to her son.

"No, honey, Luke isn't going to be your stepdad." She couldn't quite meet Luke's eyes, although she intended to ask him later just what the hell he'd thought he was doing in her bed. "I wasn't feeling well last night and Luke was nice enough to stay with me."

"But he'd make a good stepdad, Mom. He makes good pancakes and hot dogs and he cleans the horse stalls real good. I think we should marry him."

"And I think you should go make your bed and get dressed for the day," Abby replied sternly.

"Okay." Cody crawled off the bed and took off running down the hallway. "Hey, Aunt Belinda...Luke slept in Mom's bed last night," he announced as he ran.

"I'm sorry," Abby said, finally looking at Luke, who had the expression of a deer caught in a headlight beam.

He swallowed and forced a smile. "No, I'm sorry. I began the night in the chair next to the bed, but halfway through my back started hurting so I crawled into bed."

Abby smoothed the front of her T-shirt. "It happened again last night, didn't it? I went crazy."

"Yeah, but I think I've figured out what's…" He stopped midsentence as Belinda poked her head in the room.

"Everything all right?" Belinda looked at her sister worriedly.

"Fine," Abby replied, her cheeks warming beneath her sister's scrutiny. "I was ill last night. Luke stayed with me. It's no big deal."

"Want me to start breakfast?" Belinda asked, her gaze still curious on Abby.

"That would be fine," Abby agreed, embarrassed by the entire scene.

When Belinda left, Abby turned back to Luke. "Now, what were you saying?"

"I need to talk to you, but I want to run a couple of errands first. Can I borrow your pickup to go into town?"

Abby grabbed her purse from the dressertop and withdrew her keys. "You want to tell me what you're up to?"

He hesitated then shook his head. "Not yet. We'll talk later, when I get back from town." He leaned down and picked up her cocoa mix tin from the floor by the side of the bed.

"What are you doing with that?"

"Where do you get this, Abby?"

"A store on Main Street. It's called Heavenly Brews. Why?"

"I've got a hunch. Like I said, we'll talk when I get back."

She wanted to ask him a million questions, but

could tell by his expression that he was eager to get on with whatever business he had to attend to. Besides, she wanted him to leave, needed to distance herself from the memory of her first waking moments in his arms. As Cody had gone running down the hall, Abby had realized she had to make a decision.

It stewed in her head as she and Cody and Belinda ate breakfast. After they were finished Cody ran out to find Bulldog and Abby helped her sister clear the table.

"You're awfully quiet," Belinda observed as she leaned against the cabinets and eyed Abby in speculation.

"I've got a lot on my mind." Abby sighed and sank down at the table. "I'm going to ask Luke to leave today."

"Why?" Belinda joined her at the table. "I thought he was helping you figure out what was going on. I thought maybe something special was going on between the two of you."

Abby rubbed her forehead, where a headache pounded a dull but constant rhythm. "I...he has been helping me and we both want the same thing...to find out who's responsible for Greg's death. But things are getting all mixed up."

"What things? I'm not sure I understand."

Abby drew a deep breath, trying to sort out her thoughts, afraid to explore too deeply her feelings for Luke. "I'm depending on him too much. I like being with him too much. He lied to me about his identity and I don't think he believes in my innocence. I should hate him, but I can't. I...I just can't."

"You love him."

Abby wanted to protest, wanted to scream that Belinda was crazy to even think such a thing. But she couldn't. Because she knew her sister was right. As much as she didn't want it to be so, she had fallen in love with Luke Foxwood. "Yes," she answered softly, the acknowledgment pressing thickly, painfully, against her chest.

"Then why send him away?"

"It's one thing for Luke to be embroiled in my life, then walk away. But now Cody is getting involved, and I can't let it go any further."

"Are you so sure he would walk away?"

Abby nodded. "I'm positive. Luke has a life in Chicago. He's only remained here because of Greg's death. His being here has nothing to do with me and once this mess is cleared up he'll leave."

"Oh, Abby, I'm so sorry." Belinda covered Abby's hand with one of her own.

"Yeah, me, too. It's ironic—isn't it?—that finally my heart has gotten involved with a man, and that man is the half brother of my dead husband and completely inappropriate."

Again emotion ached in Abby's heart. She loved Luke. She felt it as vividly as she felt Belinda's hand on hers. And she knew she had to get him out of her life now, before she got in any deeper, before Cody's heart became too involved.

"I know Deputy Helstrom is handling the investigation of Greg's death," Luke said as he faced Junior across the table in the diner. "But I've got a couple big favors to ask of you and I'd prefer you not tell him what you're doing."

Junior frowned. "I'm not in the habit of undermining my deputies."

"Not even for Abby?" Luke held his breath, hoping he'd judged Junior right and the man wouldn't go running to Richard Helstrom.

Junior took a drink of his coffee, then raked a hand through his gray hair. "I'm not making any promises, but go ahead and tell me what you want."

Luke set Abby's cocoa tin on the tabletop. "I want this analyzed for drugs."

Junior looked at him sharply. "You think Abby is on some kind of drug?"

"I think somebody might be drugging her without her knowledge."

The sheriff tapped the top of the tin thoughtfully. "Who would do such a thing?"

"I don't know. And I can't imagine why anyone would do it. All I know for sure is that last night Abby was rational and sane before she had a cup of this stuff. After drinking it she reacted like somebody under the influence. I can't find out who put drugs in it unless I'm certain there are drugs there."

Junior took another sip of his coffee, eyeing the tin. "I suppose I could run it through the lab, see what we can find." He looked back at Luke, his gaze shrewd. "But why do you want this kept secret from Richard?"

Luke shrugged. "Call it instinct or whatever. Richard Helstrom has a vested interest in Abby being convicted."

Junior's eyes grew cold. "As far as I know, Richard is a fine police officer and wouldn't let anything personal interfere with the way he conducted a case."

"Sheriff, he might think he's being fair, but people are people and all I'm trying to do is give Abby the benefit of any doubt."

"In that we want the same thing. All right, I'll run it through the lab and won't mention it to Richard."

Luke nodded gratefully. "I have another favor to ask."

Junior winced. "What else?"

"Abby's been getting prank phone calls. The caller is Greg."

Junior barked a short laugh. "I'd say that's a little impossible. You mean it's somebody pretending to be Greg."

Luke shook his head. "No, I mean it's Greg's voice. It's happened a couple of times. I've heard it and I'm telling you it was my half brother's voice on the other end of the line."

"Don't try to convince me that we buried somebody other than Greg Foxwood. I know who we buried."

"I know Greg's dead. Since I heard the phone call it's been driving me crazy trying to figure out what's going on. I realized it has to be a tape recording of Greg's voice that somebody is playing when they call Abby. Both times it said the same thing and that's the only explanation that makes any sense."

"So, what do you want from me?"

"I want a printout from the phone company of every call Greg made from that room while he was there and to whom those calls were made."

Junior whistled and shook his head ruefully. "I don't know if that's possible. That would require a court order and as far as the court is concerned, the guilty party is already charged.''

"Surely you know somebody who can get around the legal mishmash, especially for the sake of justice.''

Junior didn't answer. He drank his coffee and stared at the wall behind Luke. "I love those Connor girls as if they were my own. When Colette was in trouble a couple months ago I did everything I could to help her, and now I'll do what I can to help Abby. I'll see what I can do about getting you that printout.'' He looked back at Luke, his gaze once again hard and cold. "There's been too much grief in those girls' lives. I hope you don't intend to add to it.''

An edge of guilt whispered through Luke as he thought of making love to Abby. He'd made love to her with no honorable intentions to back it up. He consoled himself with the thought that she hadn't expected anything from him, didn't like him enough to want anything from him. "I don't intend to stick around here long enough to cause them any more grief,'' he finally said.

Junior stared at him for a long moment, then nodded. "Good.'' He stood and picked up the cocoa tin from the top of the table. "I'll be in touch.''

Luke watched as the sheriff ambled out of the diner. Now it was just a matter of time and perhaps they'd finally have some much needed answers.

Minutes later he drove back to the ranch, eager to share with Abby what he'd done. The phone calls had been bothering him because he couldn't figure out how they'd been accomplished. He'd finally come up with the idea that somebody had taped an actual phone call from Greg and was now using a portion of that call to frighten Abby. The minute the idea had blossomed in his brain it had felt right. And going to Junior to have him follow it through also felt right. As did hurrying back to Abby's.

He frowned and eased his foot off the accelerator, slowing the truck as he admired the passing scenery. Luke had grown to love it here. It was so different from the frantic pace of Chicago, where he spent most of his days hunched over a desk and his evenings working out in the sterile atmosphere of a gym.

He'd miss this place when he left. He'd miss Abby. The thought sent shock waves through him. Although it had not been in his plans, although it was the last thing he'd wanted to happen, he realized he'd grown to care about her...deeply care.

Of course nothing would ever come of his tender desire for her. There would be no future for him here with her. He was here to find a killer, nothing more.

His mind filled with a vision of a pair of innocent, boyish blue eyes. Cody. The little boy had Greg's eyes, filled with need, a need that Luke knew he was inadequate to fill. He'd tried with Greg and he wasn't about to attempt the impossible again.

As he pulled in front of the Connor house, he shoved his thoughts, his regrets, his weaknesses aside. "Abby?" he called as he opened the back door and stepped into the kitchen. Nobody was in the kitchen although it was apparent by the clean dishes stacked in the drainer that lunch had been eaten recently.

"Abby, are you here?" he called.

"In the office," her voice drifted down the hall-way.

As Luke walked toward the office, he realized how easy it would be for somebody to step into the kitchen, add a deadly ingredient to the cocoa mix, then leave with nobody any wiser.

He found her sitting at the desk, and his heart ached as he saw the stress lines that wrinkled her forehead. "More problems?" he asked.

She nodded. "I finally got hold of my bank statement records and I'm more confused now than I was before. The checks I thought I'd written to various stores to pay bills haven't cleared yet. I can't imagine what happened to them, when they'll turn up or how much they'll be written for."

Luke sank into the chair facing the desk. "Is it possible they were made out to Greg and he didn't get a chance to cash them?"

Running a hand through her tousled curls, she sighed. "At this point anything is possible and nothing will surprise me."

"Would it surprise you if I told you I believe somebody has been drugging you?"

Her eyes flared wide and her mouth dropped open. "Wh-what are you talking about?"

"Last night you were fine until you had a cup of that hot cocoa, then you went into a completely irrational state. I don't know, I might be completely off base, but the change in you was so dramatic, so sudden, that I started wondering if perhaps the reason was something in your drink."

She stood and walked over to the window and stared out. "The night I found myself in the yard, I had a cup of hot cocoa." She turned around and looked at Luke, her eyes shining with the first glow of hope he'd seen. "But the night that Greg was murdered I didn't have any. I distinctly remember because I went to the diner for coffee and pie. Oh, Luke, if you're right, that means the night of Greg's death I didn't black out...I just fell asleep."

The light in her eyes faded, their hue deepening. "But who would do such a thing? Dear God, why would somebody do this to me?"

"Abby, we can't figure out the who or why until we make certain the cocoa really is drugged. That's what I did in town, took it to Junior, who's agreed to send it to a lab for analysis." He stood and approached her. "I also asked him to get a record of all the phone calls Greg made from his room in the weeks he was there. Hopefully in the next day or two, we'll know exactly who Greg had contact with."

"Why are you doing all this for me?" Her gaze searched his face with intensity.

He had the feeling the question stemmed from an emotion deeper than mere curiosity and he felt an involuntary need to distance himself. "I want to find my half brother's killer and I know the police have arrested the wrong person."

She nodded, but in the depths of her eyes he thought he saw a vague disappointment. "And now I need to talk to you about something," she said, any vulnerability gone from her gaze.

"About what?"

She walked over to the wall of photographs and straightened one, then another. She finally turned back to him, her eyes tumultuous with emotion. "Luke, I can't do this anymore."

"What? What can't you do?"

"Be your partner, depend on you, allow you into our lives any longer. I want you to leave the ranch."

He looked at her in confusion. "But why? Abby, we're so close to getting some answers. I need to be here, close to what's happening."

She shook her head. "I don't want you here any longer."

"But, Abby, you need me here." Odd, the dread that coursed through him at the idea of leaving. "What if you have another episode? Who's going to protect you? Keep you safe from harm?"

He could tell his words angered her. Her eyes flashed blue fire and her shoulders stiffened in protest. "If what you think is true and the cocoa is drugged, there will be no other episodes. Besides, I've lived a long time depending on myself and my sisters. I don't need you, Luke. Your presence here is only complicating things."

"Complicating things? What in the hell are you talking about?" An edge of anger built in him. He was being summarily dismissed and didn't know why.

"In case you haven't noticed, my son has taken quite a shine to you. He thinks he loves you, and he also believes you're going to become his stepdad." Her gaze bored into his, maternal protection evident in their blue depths. "You and I both know that's not about to happen. I'm not even sure I like you."

"That didn't stop you from falling into bed with me," he retorted, instantly feeling small.

"And it didn't stop you, and you still believed I was a murderer."

For a moment the air between them shimmered with regret and something more...something Luke couldn't fathom. They'd intentionally said things to hurt each other, but he had a feeling the words masked something else, something infinitely more frightening.

She sighed, her shoulders sagging in defeat. "I don't want to fight with you. I just can't allow you to stay here any longer. I don't want Cody hurt, and each day you remain here as a part of our lives will only make it more difficult on him when you finally go. Please, Luke, you have to leave before he gets hurt."

He knew she was right. It wasn't fair for him to allow Cody to believe he intended to be a part of their lives when he had no such intention at all.

Besides, there was nothing more for him to do here. It was time for him to get back to his real life and leave the justice system in charge. Hopefully with the information he'd given Junior they'd come up with a way to free her and reopen the investigation into Greg's death.

"You're right. It's time for me to go," he agreed, surprised by the sudden ache of bereavement his words caused inside him.

She released a held breath, as if she'd been waiting for something, but for what he wasn't sure. "I'll pack up my things right now," he said. He hesitated. Somehow he felt unsettled, as if there were unspoken words between them, unfinished business of some kind.

He started for the door, then hesitated and turned back to her. "Abby, I hope those midnight wishes of yours eventually come true."

She nodded, but said nothing. Luke turned and left

the office. As he walked out of the front door, Cody bounded toward him.

"Hi, Luke. Me and Bulldog are gonna go fishing. Wanna come?" The little boy gazed up at Luke, hero worship radiating in his eyes. "I'll bet you're good at fishing, huh, Luke?"

"I can't, Cody. I'm leaving to go back to Chicago." Luke steeled himself against the hurt in the childish gaze.

"But why?" Cody slipped his hand into Luke's. "I thought you liked us. I gave you my lucky nut and everything."

Cody's hand felt so small, so trusting, in Luke's. Conflicting emotions raced through him. He wanted to run as fast and as far away from this little boy. And he wanted to pick him up in his arms and hug him close to his heart.

Gently he extricated his hand and reached into his pocket. He pulled out the hickory nut Cody had given him. "Here, you'd better take this back." He held it out to the boy. "Go on, take it," he said gruffly. "Give it to a real cowboy, one who lives by your cowboy creed."

Cody took the nut, his bottom lip trembling. "But, I thought you were a real cowboy."

Again Luke had the overwhelming impulse to pick him up, hug him close and smell the sunshine freshness of his hair, the little-boy scent of dreams and innocence. He stifled the impulse and clenched his fists at his sides. "No, Cody. I'm just a pretend cowboy, and that's all I'll ever be." He turned and walked away, wondering how long Cody's disillusioned blue eyes would haunt him.

Chapter Fourteen

"You leaving?"

Luke turned to see Roger Eaton standing in the bunkhouse doorway. He nodded. "Yeah, it's time for me to move on."

"Things didn't work out between you and the boss lady?"

"As well as I expected or wanted." Luke shoved the last of his things into his duffel bag, then slammed his locker door.

"You need a ride into town? I'm heading in to pick up some things for Rusty."

"Can you drop me at the airport?" Luke asked.

"No problem."

Together the two men left the bunkhouse and headed for Rusty's old pickup. A moment later as Roger drove away from the ranch, Luke turned in his seat and cast one last glance at the house. It was past time to leave.

He was dangerously close to losing his heart to Abby and this place. But he wasn't the man for her and he'd never again attempt to raise a little boy. Better to walk away with regrets than live with them.

"I'm beginning to feel like the last rat on a sinking ship," Roger said after they had driven a few minutes in silence.

"What do you mean?" Luke looked at him curiously.

Roger shrugged. "Some of the guys were talking last night and several of them admitted they've talked to some of the other ranches in the area about potential jobs. If Abby goes to prison then we'll all be in the market for new jobs."

"So have you started scouting around?"

"Nah, my money's on Abby getting off for these murder charges. Besides, I figure the Connors have treated me square while I've been here, the least I can do is show a little loyalty and not run scared at the first sign of trouble."

Luke nodded. Although he didn't know Roger well, his respect for the wiry cowboy had just grown tenfold. He smiled inwardly as he remembered what Dotty had said about Roger telling her he was the son of some rich, important man. In his younger days Luke had thrown more than a few lines himself, but never one so creative.

"Where's home, Roger?"

"Wherever I hang my hat."

"No family?"

Roger shook his head. "Not unless you consider a series of foster homes family."

"That's rough."

"It wasn't so bad."

The men fell silent once again. Luke could better understand now Roger's painting a fantasy about his father to impress Dotty. But Luke had never spun fantasies about his father, the man who had walked out of his life when he was about Cody's age, leaving an ache of emptiness in his wake. The same emptiness Cody must feel to want a daddy so badly.

He frowned, knowing he couldn't leave town yet. He'd thought he could get on a plane and go back to Chicago, let the authorities deal with Greg's death, but he couldn't.

Somehow he'd managed to get emotionally embroiled with Abby and her son, and he couldn't walk away from them until he knew for sure they were safe.

Curiosity, that's all it is, he tried to tell himself. After all, he'd given the cocoa to Junior to be analyzed and he'd requested the phone records from Greg's room. It seemed only right he stick around to get the results and find out if his hunches were correct.

"Forget the airport," he told Roger, his mind made up. "You can just drop me off at the first motel you see."

Roger looked at him in surprise. "You aren't leaving town?"

"Not yet."

Roger shot him a look of speculation. "I heard you're Foxwood's half brother. I guess if I were you I wouldn't want to leave until somebody was in jail for the murder."

"Not just somebody. I want to make sure the right person is in jail."

Roger nodded and pulled into the parking lot of the Owl's Nest Motel. "It's nothing fancy, but I've heard it's clean and has kitchenettes,'' he said as he came to a stop.

"I'm sure it will be fine." Luke stepped out of the cab and leaned in the window. "Thanks for the ride." With a wave of his hand, he stepped back and watched as Roger pulled onto the road.

When the pickup had disappeared, Luke turned and headed for the motel office. Within minutes he was ensconced in room number ten. Just as Roger had said, the room was nothing fancy, but adequate, and in any case Luke didn't intend to be here long.

He walked to the window and pulled back the heavy, dark draperies. Staring out the window, he tried to focus on the view, but his mind filled with a vision of Abby as he'd last seen her. So strong, so independent, yet there had been a whisper of vulnerability in her eyes. Although he'd wanted to tell her not to push him out, that she needed him because he seemed to be one of the few who believed she might be innocent, she'd used the one argument with him that he couldn't fight against. Cody.

He dropped the draperies in front of the windows, effectively blocking the sunlight. The last thing he'd want to do was hurt Cody. That's why it was better this way, that he keep his distance from both the little boy and Abby until Greg's murder was solved and Luke returned to Chicago.

He thought of his apartment at home. It was not so terribly different from this motel room. Functional, adequate, but cold and without any warmth or personality. And that reflected his life.

He'd made a conscious choice long ago to live his life alone. His experiences with Greg made him wary of ever having children and his parents' broken marriage had stolen any belief in love forevermore.

Someday Abby would find the man who would make her midnight wishes come true. She'd find a man who'd love her, help her raise Cody and share all the hope deep in her heart. But that man wasn't him.

With a weary sigh, Luke stretched out on the bed, his heart filled with a deep ache. *It's grief over Greg's death catching up with me,* he thought. But he couldn't explain why when he closed his eyes, his mind filled with a vision of Abby and the pain only deepened.

"WHAT DO YOU NEED, Michael?" Abby looked up from her paperwork.

Michael Kimbers, one of the ranch workers, stood in the doorway, hat in hand. "Uh...I'm giving you my notice. I'll be leaving at the end of the week."

Dismay swept through Abby. "Is there a problem? I mean, you've been with us for—what?—almost a year."

Michael's face reddened slightly and he worked the rim of his hat between nervous fingers. "No problems. I just received another offer of employment."

"May I ask from whom?" There had always been an unwritten code among the ranchers in the area that luring workers from one ranch to another wasn't done.

"Henry Carsworth. He's offered me near double what you're paying me."

Anger swept through Abby. "But Henry Carsworth doesn't have a ranch."

Michael nodded. "I know, but he told me he expects to have something in the next couple of weeks. In the meantime he has some other work lined up for me to do." The young man smiled apologetically. "I'm sorry, Miss Abby, but I can't turn my back on that kind of money."

Abby drew a deep breath and stood. Walking around the desk, she held her hand out to Michael. "I understand. But you know there's always a place here for you if things don't work out with Mr. Carsworth."

"I appreciate that." Michael released her hand, then with a nod, turned and left.

Abby swallowed hard and turned toward the window. Damn Henry Carsworth. He was attempting to tighten the noose around her neck, shove the gasping ranch into the abyss of failure.

She stared out the window at the place she loved, the place where her heart would always be no matter what the future brought. Although now her heart would forever be divided between this ranch and Luke.

Closing her eyes, she remembered waking that morning and the emptiness that had swept through her as she thought of Luke's absence. Despite her resolve, he'd become a part of her life.

She couldn't forget their lovemaking and cursed him for reawakening those feelings in her. Luke had reminded her that she was a woman, with a woman's needs. And what she needed most was for him to love her.

She shook her head and returned to the desk, but her thoughts remained distant from the work at hand.

She'd done the right thing in sending him away. Although Cody had been hurt to discover Luke was leaving, his hurt was minimal to what it would have been had Luke remained. Yes, she'd done the right thing.

"Abby?"

She jumped as her sister came into the room. "Oh, you scared me half to death."

"Sorry." Belinda flashed her a smile of concern. "Are you all right?" She sat in the chair opposite the desk.

"I'm fine. I just wish things were different."

"You're talking about Luke."

Abby nodded. "When Greg left, I swore I'd never get involved with another man. I had Cody. I had you and Colette. I had this ranch, and I was so certain that was enough to completely fulfill me."

"You've always been the strongest, the most independent of the three of us," Belinda said. "But, Abby, everyone needs somebody special."

"I know, but it doesn't matter how I feel about Luke. He left yesterday to go back to Chicago."

"And you didn't tell him that you are in love with him?"

Abby looked at her sister as if she'd lost her mind. "Why on earth would I do something like that?"

"So that you wouldn't have any regrets later." Belinda's cheeks pinkened attractively. "I've always been sorry that I never told Derek how I felt about him. I've always wondered if telling him I loved him would have changed things between us and he might have stayed here."

"But that's different," Abby protested. "You and

Derek dated, you had a real relationship. Luke and I had a relationship based on lies. He was here for one thing and one thing only, to find me guilty of Greg's death.''

"But he no longer thinks you're guilty."

"It doesn't matter. Oh, Belinda, don't you understand? Love never had anything to do with me and Luke. I was a fool to allow things to go as far as they did between us. And there's a part of me that hates him for letting things get so out of control." She thought of the taste of Luke's lips, the heat of his hands stroking her body. She shook her head. "In any case, it's too late. He's gone." Again the emptiness rang hollowly through Abby's heart.

"Speaking of gone...I'm taking Shadow over to the Walley ranch later this afternoon. They think they might be interested in buying him."

"That would be great." Shadow was a fine Arabian horse and his sale should bring a fair price.

"I thought I'd take Cody with me. He always likes visiting the Walleys'. Okay with you if he comes with me?"

"Fine." Abby stood. "Let's go get some lunch. I'm tired of twisting numbers and trying to make our bottom line better than it is."

"It will be great to have Colette and Hank home tomorrow," Belinda said as the two sisters worked side by side to get lunch on the table.

"They should be here first thing in the morning. I just wish they were coming home to better news."

"Abby, things will be okay. You know Mama used to always say it's darkest before the dawn."

"It's been dark a long time and I see no hint of the dawn," Abby replied ruefully.

As the afternoon waned on, the darkness seemed only to thicken. Two more ranch hands came to Abby to put in their notices, stolen away by Henry Carsworth's bulging wallet and big promises.

When Belinda and Cody left with the prize horse in the trailer, Abby sat on the front porch, exhausted of spirit. Up until now she'd managed to hold on to a modicum of hope that they could save the ranch, that somehow they'd get a lucky break. Now even hope seemed a luxury she couldn't afford.

If they lost the ranch, she knew Colette and Hank would be all right. Hank was a good man, and he'd do whatever it took to provide for his wife and daughter. He'd quit his job to help with the ranch, but he could always go back to law enforcement.

Belinda worried Abby. Belinda had tried living away from the ranch for a while, but had hated it. This ranch was as much a part of her as it was of Abby. And like Abby, a piece of Belinda's soul would die if they lost the ranch.

Abby steadfastly refused to think of where she might be or what she might do if they no longer had their home. For all she knew, a prison might be her address for the next hundred years of her life. And that possibility was too grim to consider.

The ranch was quiet for the moment. No ringing hammers, masculine shouts, nothing to break the peace and serenity of evening's approach. It was Friday night; most of the men would have already left the ranch for a night out on the town.

Abby listened to the lullaby of nature, the stir of

the warm breeze through distant trees, a bird's song as it flew overhead, a buzz of a bee seeking a plump flower. How long did she have to enjoy these simple things? Would she be able to remember them from a jail cell?

The sun had just begun its descent, painting the sky with orange and pink streaks when a cloud of dust announced a car's approach.

Abby stood, steeling herself mentally for whoever it might be and whatever news they might bring. She used to look forward to company, enjoyed entertaining people in her home. It saddened her to realize that in the space of the last couple of weeks, she'd changed so drastically, now certain company meant bad news.

As the small red economy car came into view, she didn't recognize it. But as it pulled to a stop and the driver's door opened, surprise shot through her.

"I thought you'd gone back to Chicago," she said to Luke as he got out of the car. She tried to ignore how achingly handsome he looked, the quickening in her heart as he stepped up on the porch.

"I decided to stick around for a little while longer."

"Morbid curiosity?" she asked.

He smiled. "Perhaps, and a need for closure where Greg's case is concerned."

She nodded, unable to fault him for that. If one of her sisters had been murdered, she'd want to see it through, make certain the guilty was punished. "Where are you staying?"

"Owl's Nest Motel." He moved closer to her, his

gaze intent as he scanned her features. "You look tired."

"I am." She almost resented his observation. She resented that he knew her well enough to know she looked tired, yet couldn't see the fact that she was helplessly in love with him. "I had three men quit today."

His dark eyebrows raised in surprise. "Why?"

"Henry Carsworth. He hired them away from me."

"Did he buy a place around here?"

Abby sighed. "From what I understand, not yet. He seems to be certain he's going to get this place before long." She wrapped her arms around herself and stared out at the landscape, cold despite the heat of the summer evening. "I feel like a rabbit waiting for the hawk to dive toward me." She looked at Luke once again. "So, what brings you back here?"

"I saw Junior this morning. Yesterday he took your cocoa mix to a lab and he should have the results sometime in the next couple of days. He also told me before he requested any phone records from Greg's room, he wants a copy of the tape you made. You still have it?"

Abby nodded. "I put it in the office." But she didn't move to get it. Instead her conversation with Belinda replayed in her mind. If she didn't tell Luke how she felt about him, would she always wonder? Always regret?

"Abby, it's possible in the next day or two we'll have enough information to vindicate you," Luke said as he took a step closer to her.

She looked at him, studying his face, loving each and every feature that made him who he was. "And is that important to you? There was a time when you were certain I was guilty.''

"That was before I knew you, when I only had Greg's perceptions to form my opinion. Abby, certainly it's important to me that you don't go to prison for a crime you didn't commit.''

In his eyes she saw the whisper of an emotion that gave her hope, buoyed courage through her. She leaned toward him and placed her palm against his cheek. "Luke, don't go back to Chicago. Stay here. Stay here with me.''

His eyes flamed with heat at her touch and she heard his breath catch in his chest. For a moment she couldn't speak. The words she wanted to say to him were filled with emotion too huge. His hand covered hers on his cheek. "I love you, Luke. God help me, I don't want to, but I do. I want you to be the man in my life. I want my dreams to come true with you at my side.''

"Abby." He whispered her name with a wealth of regret that seemed at odds with the expression on his face. Gently he removed her hand from his cheek and stepped back from her. "I never intended for this to happen.''

"Neither did I," Abby replied, a dull ache sweeping through her as he took another step back from her.

"Abby, you just think you love me because I've supported you through these rough times. It's only natural you'd feel a certain fondness for me.''

She stared at him, anger riveting through her. "How dare you. How dare you try to tell me what I feel and why. How dare you minimize my feelings because I've obviously made you uncomfortable by speaking of them.''

He raked a hand through his hair and averted his gaze from hers. "You're right." He walked over to the railing and stood with his back to her. "But it doesn't matter how you feel about me, or what I feel for you. There's more involved here."

Again hope filled Abby's heart. Of course he was reluctant to bind himself to a woman with a court case hanging over her head. "But, Luke, you said yourself hopefully Junior will come up with some answers that will help vindicate me. Once we get this court mess behind us, we could make a go of the ranch."

She drew a deep breath. "Can you honestly look me in the eyes and tell me you don't feel something for me? That you don't love me?"

He turned back to her, his eyes darkened with pain. "No, Abby, I can't honestly tell you I don't love you." He sighed wearily. "I came here hating you, believing you were a coldhearted woman. And I'm leaving here loving you, but I am leaving."

"But why?" She searched his features, needing to understand, joy battling with pain.

He clenched his hands into fists. "Because I can't be the man you need. I can't be the man Cody needs."

"Cody?" Again confusion swirled inside Abby. "What does he have to do with this? Cody loves you."

"Cody needs a man to be his father, just like Greg needed years ago. I blew it with Greg, and I won't make the same mistake with your son. I'll live the rest of my life with guilt over the fact that I let Greg down. I couldn't live with that same kind of guilt where Cody is concerned.''

"You're afraid." Abby stared at him incredulously. "You're afraid of Cody's love."

He didn't answer and again he averted his gaze. "I promised my father when he died that I'd do the right thing by Greg, raise him to be a good man. I failed miserably. Cody needs a man who knows how to be a father."

"Luke, you told me Greg was sixteen years old when he came to live with you. By that age he'd already developed into the man he became. No matter how much you loved him, guided him, tried to help him, he was what he was. Cody needs a man who will love him. That's all he needs.''

He looked her right in the eyes. "I'm not willing to take on a child. I love you, Abby, but I won't become a part of your life. I'd be no good to Cody, and eventually that would make me no good to you."

She wanted to scream at him, use common sense to pound him over the head. Cody wasn't Greg and never would become a man like Greg. But she saw in Luke's stance, in his eyes, that it didn't matter what she said. He intended to turn his back on her and walk out of her life because he was afraid.

"I'll go get the tape," she said dully. She turned to go into the house, but hesitated as Luke caught her arm.

"Abby, I'm sorry." Emotion thickened, deepened his voice.

"For what?" She gazed at him dispassionately, all hope dead, all dreams lost. "Sorry for being man enough to bed me, but not man enough to stay with me, build a life with me? Don't worry, Luke. I'll get over it.'' She pulled her arm from his grasp and went into the house.

As she walked down the hallway toward the office, she refused to give in to the tears that burned, threatening to overwhelm her. He loved her...but not enough to overcome his fear. It seemed that even beyond the grave Greg's legacy to her continued to be one of unhappiness.

She entered the office and froze in the doorway. Rusty stood behind the desk, the checkbook open in front of him.

"Rusty?"

He jumped, obviously startled by her sudden appearance. "Oh, uh, I was just..."

"Rusty, not you." Abby had thought her heart incapable of any more pain, but as she looked at the man who'd worked for them for so many years, a man she'd trusted beyond doubt, her heart found a new place to ache.

"You've been stealing checks and forging my name." It wasn't a question, it was knowledge. Knowledge gleaned from the hatred that radiated from his eyes as he glared at her. "Why, Rusty?"

"Why? Because you owe me. I should own this place." He appeared to grow younger, more alive with his rage. "I've put fifteen years of my sweat into this ranch and I've got nothing to show for it. I've just been taking what I deserve."

"You've been bleeding us dry." Anger swiftly overrode the pain. "You're going to jail, Rusty."

Rusty laughed. "For what? Nobody is gonna believe you. Everyone's talking about how confused you've been, how you haven't been yourself at all lately. Nobody is going to believe whatever you say."

Fear swept through her as she realized he might be right.

"They'll believe me." Luke stepped into the room. "Abby, call Deputy Helstrom and get him out here. I think we're about to get some much needed answers."

Chapter Fifteen

"Have a seat, Rusty. I'm not letting you out of here until you're in Helstrom's custody," Luke said as he pointed to the chair behind the desk.

The old man sank into the chair, once again looking old and defeated. "Deputy Helstrom is on his way," Abby said as she hung up the phone receiver.

Luke stared at the old man. "It's over now, Rusty."

"It ain't over till it's over," Rusty returned.

"You wrote those checks to Greg, didn't you?" Abby asked. Luke could tell by the pallor of her cheeks how hard Rusty's betrayal had hit her. He refused to consider that her paleness might be a result of their conversation moments before.

"Greg was a stupid, greedy man," Rusty exclaimed angrily. "He found out I had access to the checks, and demanded he get cut into some of the action."

"And when you tired of paying him, you killed him." Luke's blood ran cold in his veins as he stared at the foreman. He'd always known Greg's greed had probably gotten him killed, but there had been another human being on the opposite end of that branding iron and as Luke looked into Rusty's eyes, he saw the eyes of his half brother's killer. "You killed Greg, didn't you?"

"I don't see a lawyer present, so I reckon I don't have to answer any of your questions." He crossed his arms and leaned back in the chair.

"Did you try to hurt me by throwing a bale of hay from the loft?" Abby asked.

Rusty looked at her in surprise. "I don't know what you're talking about."

"You didn't throw a bale of hay or put a tack under Blackheart's saddle blanket in an effort to hurt me?" Abby's gaze remained intent on Rusty.

"I didn't do anything like that."

"But you did drug her cocoa," Luke interjected.

Rusty's eyes flared wide, then narrowed, and again he clamped his mouth tightly shut, indicating he wasn't about to incriminate himself in anything that couldn't be proven.

"We'll know the truth soon enough," Luke said. "It's only a matter of time and you're going to be behind bars."

A small smile crept across Rusty's lips. "We'll see when all is said and done who's where."

Something about the smile caused an uneasiness to ripple through Luke. What did the old man have up his sleeve? Luke knew in his gut, in the very core of his being, that Rusty had killed Greg. And the fact that it had apparently been over money only added to the indignity of death.

Restlessly he moved over to the window, wondering what in the hell was keeping Deputy Helstrom.

Abby'd caught Rusty with his hand in the till. At the very least Rusty would face a charge of theft. But Luke wanted more. He wanted Rusty behind bars for Greg's death.

He turned and looked at Abby. She stood in the doorway, as if, should Rusty decide to make a run for it, she'd physically barricade him from escape. Her color had returned, firing her cheeks with her ire.

His heart had always known she was innocent. Despite the evidence against her, his heart had known the truth. His gaze met hers across the room and in hers he saw not only love but a vast relief. He realized then that until this moment she hadn't been one hundred percent convinced of her own innocence. He walked across the room to stand next to her.

"It's almost over, Abby," he said softly. He kept his voice low enough so Rusty couldn't hear him. "Rusty will break. He'll confess to killing Greg and everything else he's responsible for. He's an old man. He'll cooperate for a lesser sentence."

She nodded. "And I'll have my life back." She looked up at him. "And you can go home knowing the real killer is behind bars."

Home. Yes, he could go back to Chicago, although he had a feeling it would never feel like home again. Home was here with Abby, holding her in his arms, loving her with every fiber of his being.

But no matter how much he loved her, he couldn't forget that this entire situation was partially his fault. Had he done his job in guiding Greg, none of this would have happened.

A knock resounded on the front door. "That must be Richard. I'll go let him in," Abby said.

As she left the room, once again a small smile curved Rusty's lips and another wave of uneasiness crept through Luke. He had a feeling the old coot had something up his sleeve, but for the life of him, Luke couldn't figure out what it might be.

"What's going on in here?" Richard Helstrom entered the office with Abby just behind him. He eyed Luke, then Rusty.

"I walked into the office and surprised Rusty stealing checks from my checkbook," Abby said.

Richard looked at Rusty with disgust. "You stupid old fool."

"That's not all. We also think Rusty is responsible for Greg's death," Luke added.

"I am. I did kill Greg." Rusty came alive with his confession, his eyes flaming anger as he sat up straight in the chair. "He was nothing but a mewling, greedy pain. Once he discovered I was dipping my hand into the till, he demanded a cut of the action."

"And after you paid him a couple thousand, you got tired and killed him." Luke kept his voice cool and controlled despite the pain and anger that rippled through him.

"I went to his room to tell him to leave town, that he'd bled me enough. But he laughed at me, told me he wasn't near half done collecting money." Rusty's faded eyes flashed darkly. "He pushed me, told me I was just an old man and I'd better do as he told me. I went out to my truck, got a branding iron and killed him."

"Rusty, why don't you shut up," Richard snapped. He pulled his revolver from his holster.

Abby gasped when instead of aiming it at Rusty,

he aimed it at Luke. "I'm afraid Rusty has a big mouth and now it seems you and Miss Abby here have become liabilities."

Luke stared at the lawman, his brain unable to comprehend this sudden twist of events. "You're working together? You and Rusty?"

Rusty stood and walked over to Richard. He clapped him on the back and smiled at Luke. "Oh, guess I forgot to mention that Richard here is my son. Remember I told you about him. Seems he got a wild hair and decided to look up his old man."

"Although dear old dad here wasn't supposed to get caught filching checks," Richard said.

"This has never been about the small amounts of money you could misappropriate, it's about the ranch, isn't it?" Luke said.

Richard motioned for Abby to join Luke in the center of the room. As she moved beside him, Luke placed an arm around her, felt the shivers that rippled through her. "You're right," Richard replied.

"I—I don't understand," Abby said.

"They've been stealing your money, Abby. I'd imagine initially they hoped to force you into selling because you couldn't afford to do anything else. Then Greg was killed and they saw an opportunity to make certain you lost the ranch by framing you for his murder."

"Very good." Richard flashed Luke a tight smile. "Nobody was supposed to die, but Dad has a bad temper and Greg was not a nice person. Dad spiked Abby's cocoa with a little hallucinogenic, figuring she'd start acting weird and make it easier for everyone to believe she'd killed Greg. I pulled the button off her blouse the day I arrested her. It only took me a minute to go back and add in one bloody button to the crime scene report."

Luke prayed for a moment when the gun might waver, when Richard would be distracted enough to get the sight of the gun off him and Abby. But Richard appeared cool and completely in control. As he spoke about what he and Rusty had done, a feeling of doom engulfed Luke. There was no way the two criminals would walk out of here and leave Luke and Abby alive, not after telling them everything that had been done.

"Rusty, go get some rope," Richard said.

Abby shivered again and Luke pulled her tighter against his side, wishing he could figure out how to get her out of here, out of danger's way.

"You'll never get away with this, Helstrom," Luke said.

Richard's eyebrows danced upward and he smiled wryly. "I can't imagine who can stop us."

"What are you going to do with us?" Abby asked as Rusty returned with a long coil of rope.

"There's going to be a tragic accident." Keeping the gun pointed directly at Abby, Richard moved the chair from behind the desk and put it back-to-back with the straight-backed chair in front of the desk. He motioned for Abby and Luke to each have a seat.

As they sat, back-to-back, Rusty began by first tying their hands behind them, then winding the rope around the two chairs, binding them together.

While Rusty tied them securely, Richard began throwing crumpled papers into the metal wastebasket by the side of the desk. "Did you know that in most home fires, victims don't die from the flames, but rather succumb to smoke inhalation?" he said as he continued to fill the trash can.

Luke's blood ran cold as he realized their intentions. He felt Abby's fear emanating from her even though he couldn't see her face and knew she also realized what they planned to do.

"Rusty, get out of here. Go someplace where you'll be seen by people to establish an alibi," Richard said as he pulled a book of matches from his breast pocket.

"This will never work, Helstrom. Somebody will see the flames in the night," Luke said.

Richard smiled, a cold, killer gesture. "I know how to set a fire to get maximum smoke and minimal flame. By the time anyone knows you're in here, it will be too late."

"I'll meet you tonight at Wild Coyote's," Rusty said to Richard, then he disappeared out the door.

For a moment there was silence except for the sound of Abby's frantic breathing as she struggled against the ropes that bound her.

"I'm sorry it's got to be this way. I never intended for anyone to get hurt, but I suppose when you get lemons you make lemonade," Richard said.

"What are you going to tell people to explain our deaths?" Abby asked. "Don't you think people will get suspicious under the circumstances?"

"You've forgotten, Abby. We're rural out here. I'll make sure I'm the one to investigate the fire." He leaned against the desk, his expression as bland as if he were talking about the weather. "The way I figure it, Abby was a careless smoker." He pulled a pack of cigarettes from his pocket and shook one out.

"That's crazy, I don't smoke," Abby protested.

"Yes, you do. I can testify that when I interrogated you right after your arrest, you smoked one cigarette after another. Rusty will be able to tell everyone he saw you sneaking cigarettes several times. He'll also be able to tell everyone that you just weren't quite right in the head for the last couple of months. You even mentioned getting phone calls from Greg long after his funeral." He lit the cigarette and took a deep drag. "Yeah, the way I see it, your smoking carelessness caused two tragic deaths." He threw the cigarette into the wastebasket. "This is really for the best. Abby, your sisters will mourn you deeply, and in their grief they'll sell the ranch and I'll buy it for me and my father. We'll think of you often with fondness."

He smiled as smoke swirled out of the wastebasket, and in his smile Luke saw the cold absence of conscience, the trait of a sociopath.

With his foot, he moved the wastebasket closer to the love seat against the back wall, where once the smoldering burst into flames, they could easily consume the fabric. Casting a final smile at his two victims, he left the room, softly closing the door behind him.

The minute he left, Luke struggled against the ropes that tightly crisscrossed his chest. "Dammit," he gasped after several moments of exertion. "Who'd have thought that scrawny old man could tie such tight knots?"

"I can't believe this. I can't believe any of this is happening."

Luke heard the edge of hysteria in Abby's voice and wished he could hold her, assure her that everything would be fine. But, of course, not only could he not hold her, but he had little hope to offer her.

He struggled once again, attempting to free himself from the ropes, but there was no give. The room was quickly filling with smoke, a thick black smoke that burned the back of his throat and stung his eyes. "Dammit," he repeated helplessly.

"Help. Help us," Abby screamed, but her scream ended with another harsh round of coughing.

Flames leapt out of the wastebasket and licked the edge of the sofa, blackening the fabric and creating more thick smoke.

Abby coughed, a wrenching sound that tore at Luke's heart. "Abby, I'm so sorry. I should have realized. I knew there was something not right, that Rusty had something up his sleeve. I should have done something. I should have sensed the danger."

"Shut up, Luke. Just shut up. Stop trying to take responsibility for everything that happens." She paused and choked again, then continued, her voice deeper, more harsh. "This isn't your fault. Greg wasn't your fault. Stop beating yourself up and help me figure out a way to get us out of this mess."

The harsh tickle in the back of Luke's throat prevented him from saying anything else. Instead he closed his eyes against the burn of the smoke and wondered if his last thoughts on this earth would be ones tinged with regret.

ABBY HAD NEVER been so hot. The sofa had burst into flames moments before and for the first time since Rusty had tied them to the chair, Abby realized she was going to die. Her lungs ached with each breath and perspiration dappled the surface of her skin as the heat in the room intensified.

"Help! Please, somebody!" Her throat was raw and she knew there was no way anyone would hear their cries for help above the fire's growl.

It seemed ironic that she would die tied to a man who professed to love her, but not enough to devote the rest of his life to her. Now in death they would be bound through eternity.

She coughed again, fighting for breath in the noxious smoke. Her home was burning, she and the man she loved were probably mere minutes from death. It couldn't end this way, it just couldn't.

She strove to free her hands, twisting and turning until her wrists felt raw. She knew Luke attempted the same, could feel his frantic movements as he fought against the rope that held them.

An involuntary scream erupted from her raw throat as the curtains caught fire, the flames licking up toward the ceiling. Terror screamed inside her as she felt the hot breath of death surrounding her.

She stopped struggling, realizing her efforts were useless. Closing her eyes against the stinging hot ash and the black soot that swirled in the air, she felt the last gasp of hope leave her body.

Luke touched her hand, his fingers entwining with hers. "Abby." He gasped her name above the din of the snapping, crackling, roaring fire. "Abby, I do love you."

Tears burned as they oozed down her cheeks. His words soothed her fear, gave her the peace and courage to face what Fate had in store for them.

"I love you, Luke," she answered, the words coming with difficulty from her scorched lungs. She could no longer see anything in the room but flames and thick black smoke. Luke's fingers tightened around hers and she closed her eyes once again and waited for death.

"Miss Abby! Are you in there?"

Abby opened her eyes, feeling as if she were coming out of a dream. She realized she'd momentarily passed out and from the tightness of the rope, she assumed Luke had slumped into unconsciousness. "Hello? Is somebody there?"

"Miss Abby. You got to get out of there." Bulldog's voice rang from the doorway.

"Bulldog, we need help. We're tied. Get a knife and cut us free," Abby screamed.

Seconds passed, long seconds as unconsciousness once again flirted with Abby, attempting to pull her under into the blackness of oblivion. The doorway where Bulldog had appeared was on fire and she wondered how he'd get into the room to cut them loose. Any sane, rational person would not try to get through the flaming doorway.

"He'll have to find another way in," Luke yelled, and Abby realized at some point he'd regained consciousness.

"The window is on fire, too," Abby said, hope again seeping away.

"I'm coming, Miss Abby," Bulldog's voice rang from the hallway.

"No, Bulldog, it's too dangerous," Luke yelled.

With a roar of sheer emotion, Bulldog burst through the flaming doorway and rushed to where Abby and Luke were tied. Using a kitchen knife, he sawed through the rope. Abby gasped in relief as she felt herself freed from the chair.

"Don't worry about our hands," Luke exclaimed. "Let's just get the hell out of here." He started for the doorway, but intense heat drove him back.

"Don't worry, Miss Abby. Follow me." Before Abby could stop him, Bulldog ran for the window and threw himself through. As the fresh air flooded in, the fire intensified, fed by the oxygen.

"Go!" Luke yelled, and he pushed her toward the opening Bulldog had made.

Within minutes they were out, gasping and choking as they drew in the sweet night air. In the distance the wail of sirens rose above the din of the fire.

"I called them from the kitchen," Bulldog said. He looked at Abby. "I told them we needed help. That was a good thing to do, wasn't it?"

Abby cupped Bulldog's face in her hands. His features were blackened with soot, and scratches and cuts bled freely from his plunge through the window. "That wasn't just a good thing to do, it was the smart thing to do." A smile wreathed his face. "You saved our lives, Bulldog."

"'Course I did. You're my family, Miss Abby. I love all of you."

She hugged him. She knew other men would have been smart enough to be too afraid to first run into a flaming room, then throw themselves through a window. Bulldog hadn't reacted from intelligence, he'd acted from love.

As she released Bulldog, Luke pulled her into his arms. "Thank God you're all right," he breathed into her hair.

She nodded and stepped out of his embrace as two fire trucks pulled in front of the house and half a dozen firemen set to work. Yes, she was all right, but her house was burning and the man she loved would soon be gone from her life.

"Mom!"

She turned at the sound of Cody's voice. As Belinda pulled the truck to a stop, Cody bounded from the passenger seat. He threw himself into her arms, wrapping his legs around her waist as he held her tight around the neck.

"It's okay, Cody. I'm all right." She squeezed him tight, frightened as she realized how close she'd come to never seeing him again, never holding him again.

Cody released his hold on her neck and looked at her. "Your face is all black. Were you in the fire?"

"Yes, sweetheart, but I'm okay now." Abby smiled as Belinda rushed to her side.

"Was Luke in the fire, too?"

Abby nodded. "But he's okay."

For a few minutes the two sisters watched as the firemen worked to put out the flames. Abby continued to hold Cody, who seemed to sense her need and didn't fight what would normally be the unwanted display of motherly affection.

"Abby." She turned to see Luke. "I'm going with Junior." He gestured to where the sheriff had parked and appeared to be waiting for Luke. "We're going after Rusty and Richard. Will you be all right?"

She looked at him, memorizing his features to sustain her on long lonely nights. "Of course." She hugged her son. "Cody and I are going to be just fine."

She could tell by the expression in his eyes that he'd gotten her point. He could leave now, go back to Chicago and his life. She and Cody were a package deal, and if he couldn't love her son, she didn't want his love.

For another long moment their gazes remained connected, then he nodded curtly, as if he'd heard all the thoughts in her head. "Goodbye, Abby." He turned to leave.

"Hey, Luke." Cody wiggled out of his mother's embrace and ran after him.

Luke paused, his gaze curious as he eyed the little boy. Cody dug into his pocket and pulled out the good luck hickory nut. "Even though you're not a real cowboy, I still like you. You'd better take this. If you'd had it before probably you wouldn't have been in the fire."

Abby was too far away to see Luke's expression, but her heart broke as she watched her son give his good luck charm and his love to a man who apparently couldn't return that love.

Luke took the nut and without a backward glance walked away. Abby watched as he got into the patrol car with Junior. Cody ran back to her, his gaze also going to the patrol car driving away. "We aren't going to see Luke again, are we?"

"No, honey. I don't think so."

"I think he could have been a real cowboy if he'd tried harder, don't you?" Cody asked.

Abby squeezed her son's shoulders sympathetically, unable to speak around the lump of emotion in her throat.

Chapter Sixteen

Dawn brought a nightmare sight. In the early glow of morning light the full extent of the damage to the house was evident. Abby sat on the bench next to the barn, staring at the gaping black hole that marred the exterior of her home.

She should be grateful. Although it had taken most of the night, the firemen had managed to contain the fire to the office area. The rest of the house had been saved except for some smoke damage in the rooms nearest the office.

She rubbed her eyes, wondering if they were gritty from lack of sleep or the smoke that still lay heavy and black in the area.

Junior had shown up a little earlier, telling her both Rusty and Richard were behind bars. They would face a variety of charges that would keep them out of society for the rest of their lives. "I'm sorry, Abby girl," he'd said, his pain evident in his wearied voice. "I'm sorry for doubting you and not seeing the evil in Richard."

"No apology necessary," Abby had replied as

she'd hugged him. She hadn't asked about Luke, and Junior hadn't mentioned him.

She couldn't think about him now. Perhaps later she'd grieve his loss, cry for what might have been, what would never be. But at the moment she had to figure out what she was going to do.

She looked up as Belinda exited the house and walked toward her. "Here, I thought you might need this." She held out a cup of coffee.

Abby grinned ruefully. "Thanks. I don't think I'll ever want another cup of hot cocoa again." Her smile faded as Belinda joined her on the bench.

"Looks pretty dismal, doesn't it?" Belinda said softly, her gaze on the burned area.

"Yes, and I think it's the straw that has broken my back." Abby took a deep breath. "I think maybe it's best if we sell."

"Oh, Abby, no."

"Henry Carsworth will pay a good price for the place," she continued as if she hadn't heard Belinda's protest. "It would probably be the best thing to do."

"Abby, I know things look hopeless right now, but this isn't the time to be making any decisions. You've had no sleep, you've been through a trauma."

"I could sleep for days and I think I'd come to the same conclusion. Belinda, we only have enough money left to put off the inevitable. It takes money to make money, and we'll never have enough to make this a real, working, productive ranch."

"I've never heard you talk this way," Belinda replied. "You've always been so filled with hope, so full of dreams."

"It's gone. They're gone." Abby bit her bottom

lip to still the tears that pressed hotly behind her eyelids. She had a feeling Luke had taken her dreams with him and there was little he'd left behind. "As soon as Colette and Hank get back later today, we'll have a family meeting and decide what we're going to do."

Belinda nodded and stood. "I'm going to make some breakfast. Want to come in and eat?"

Abby shook her head. "No, thanks. I'm really not hungry. I just want to sit here for a while and decompress."

"Let me know if I can do anything." Belinda gave Abby a quick hug, then walked back to the house.

Abby watched the sun climb upward, her gaze alternating between the glory of the new day and the ashes of her dreams.

She finally moved, deciding to sit on the porch where her gaze would be on the land and not on the house. The land. Her father had bought this land as a young man. It had been his dream that it would be his legacy to the generations of Connors who would come after him.

She didn't know how long she'd been sitting there when she became aware of being watched. She looked first in the direction of the shed, then toward the barn.

And there he was.

He stood in the early morning shadows, in the same place where she'd first seen him a lifetime ago. His black hat was pulled low, obscuring his eyes from her scrutiny. "What are you doing here?" she asked, a deep, abiding weariness seeping through her. Why hadn't he already left town? Why the need to come here one last time?

He left the shadows next to the barn and stepped into the morning light. Ambling toward her with the loose-hipped walk that enticed her, he smiled. The devastating smile she'd come to love.

"Ma'am." He swept the dark hat off his head. "My name is Luke Foxwood and I'm here because I understand you have an opening for a cowboy."

Abby stood and wrapped her arms around herself, wondering why he was torturing her, what game he was playing with her emotions. "There are no openings here."

"What about an opening for a lover, a husband...a father."

His words hung in the air, shimmering with promise, but Abby refused to be taken in by that promise. Her heart lay too heavy, her dreams shattered into pieces. "What game are you playing, Luke? I don't have the energy or the heart to do this."

He walked to the porch and stepped up beside her. "No games, Abby. I've had most of the night to think. I could have gotten on a plane several times, but I just couldn't make myself leave. I love you, Abby." He took a step toward her, but she backed away.

"We've been through this before. We can't just think about your heart, or mine. I've got a little boy's heart to consider."

Luke nodded. He reached into his pocket and withdrew the hickory nut Cody had given him the night before. "Funny thing about this. It doesn't look so big and it easily fit into my pocket. But remember

that old fairy tale about the princess and the pea? This
nut poked and prodded me all night long, only instead
of hurting my leg, it made my heart ache.''

"Guilt," Abby said. "Or fear," she added, un-
willing to allow her own heart any hope.

"Or love."

"Oh, please," Abby scoffed. "Yesterday your love
for Cody didn't seem so overwhelming."

"Yesterday I hadn't faced death by fire, nor the
actuality of losing you, of losing a chance to build
something here."

"There's nothing left to build." Abby's voice was
empty, devoid of emotion. She recognized the hol-
lowness, felt it echoing inside her.

"Abby." He placed his hands on her shoulders,
forcing her to look at him, look into his eyes. "While
that inferno was blazing around us last night, you said
something to me that made sense."

"And what was that?"

He smiled. "You told me to shut up and stop trying
to take on the responsibility for everything that had
happened. I realize now I've carried around the guilt
that Greg should have carried, I felt responsible for
things that were not my fault.

"Abby—" he cupped her chin with his hand "—I
love you as I've never loved anyone before, but I was
afraid of taking on the responsibility of Cody. I was
afraid of his need, afraid I'd be inadequate and
couldn't fill those needs. Then last night, when he
handed me back his good luck nut, I looked in his
eyes and all I saw was love. Not need, just pure
love." His voice cracked with emotion and in his
words Abby found her faith again, her hope.

"I realized I'd be more than a fool if I walked away from you and Cody and the love we've found for each other."

"Oh, Luke." Abby's heart swelled and she wrapped her arms around his neck. "I love you."

His lips claimed hers, promising love, passion and dreams to be fulfilled. Abby pressed against him, wanting to hold him close forever. "Marry me, Abby. Marry me and let me be the man who makes those midnight wishes of yours come true."

"Yes, Luke." Tears of happiness trekked down her cheeks. "I want to spend the rest of my life with you." She saw the fires in his eyes, fires of love burning brightly, and knew this was one cowboy who would not ride off alone into the sunset.

"Hey, are you making my mom cry?"

They both turned to see Cody, who'd just stepped out of the house. He eyed Luke suspiciously.

"It's okay, Cody." Abby laughed and wiped at her tears. "I'm crying because I'm so happy."

Luke walked over to Cody and crouched down so they were eye-to-eye. "It looks like I'm going to be marrying your mother," he said.

Cody's blue eyes widened. "Does this mean you really are a real cowboy?"

"I guess it does."

Cody frowned. "But you told me you weren't a real one."

Luke looked at the little boy thoughtfully. "Do you know the story of Pinocchio?"

"The wooden puppet?" Cody nodded.

"Do you remember what made Pinocchio real?"

"Love," Cody answered without hesitation.

Luke nodded. "And that's what's made me real. Your mom loving me...and you loving me."

Cody wrapped his arms around Luke's neck and Luke returned the gesture, hugging the little boy tight. Abby watched the two males she loved and she knew she could face whatever the future held as long as they were by her side. Her wishes would come true...in fact, they already had.

Epilogue

"I still can't believe all this," Colette said as she helped straighten the back of Abby's wedding gown. "Things are usually pretty boring around here, but I go away on my honeymoon and come back to find that my sister's been arrested for murder, the house has nearly burned down and she's found the man she's going to marry."

Belinda laughed. "That will teach you to go away."

The three sisters were in Abby's bedroom. Abby stared at herself in the mirror, still unable to believe that within minutes she would become Mrs. Luke Foxwood.

It had been three weeks since he'd proposed to her, three weeks of deepening love. She'd watched as the bond between Luke and Cody had grown stronger. Three weeks of joy that she knew was merely a prelude to a lifetime of happiness and love.

"Come on, it's time," Colette said as she checked her wristwatch.

They had decided to be married beneath the dragon

tree, in the same place where a little over a month before Colette and Hank had said their vows.

Bulldog awaited with a ribbon-bedecked wagon that would carry Abby and her two sisters to where the ceremony would take place beneath the tree. Bulldog beamed at her as he helped her up into the wagon. "You look mighty pretty, Miss Abby," he said.

"Thank you, Bulldog. You look mighty handsome yourself," she replied. "The most handsome best man I've ever seen." Bulldog smiled with pride. His face still retained the burns he'd received when he'd rescued them, and his eyebrows and lashes had been singed off, but to Abby he looked like a hero.

As the wagon carried her toward her destiny, Abby took one look back at her home. The sisters had voted to try to hang on to the ranch, refusing to sell their heritage until there was no alternative left. From the exterior there was no sign of the fire, although there was still work to be done on the inside.

The charges against Abby had been dropped, and all the loose ends of Greg's death and Rusty's betrayal had been tied up. Both Rusty and Richard had continued to maintain that they'd had nothing to do with the tack under Blackheart's saddle blanket or the hay bale that had nearly killed Abby. Abby had chalked the incidents up to the hazards and accidents of ranch life.

As the wagon drew closer to the dragon tree, all thoughts left Abby's head. Beneath the tree, next to the preacher, stood Luke and Cody. Clad in matching tuxedos, the sight of them made Abby's heart swell with joy.

"Come on, Mom," Cody called impatiently. "I've been waiting a long time to get a dad. Hurry up."

Abby didn't wait for the wagon to come to a full halt. She gathered her skirt in her arms and jumped down. With a smile on her lips and in her heart, Abby ran toward her future.

Cheyenne Nights

by Carla Cassidy

As little girls the Connor sisters dreamed of gallant
princes on white horses. As women they were swept away
by mysterious cowboys on black stallions. But with dusty
dungarees and low-hung Stetsons, their cowboys are no
less the knights in shining armor.

Join Carla Cassidy for the Connor sisters'
wild West Wyoming tales of intrigue:

SUNSET PROMISES
(March)

MIDNIGHT WISHES
(April)

SUNRISE VOWS
(May)

Take 4 bestselling love stories FREE

Plus get a FREE surprise gift!

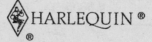

It's hot...and it's out of control!

BLAZE

Beginning this spring, Temptation turns up the *heat.* Look for these bold, provocative, *ultra*sexy books!

#629 OUTRAGEOUS
by Lori Foster (April 1997)

#639 RESTLESS NIGHTS
by Tiffany White (June 1997)

#649 NIGHT RHYTHMS
by Elda Minger (Sept. 1997)

***BLAZE:* Red-hot reads—only from**

As Seen on TV!

Free Gift Offer

With a Free Gift proof-of-purchase
from any Harlequin® book, you can receive
a beautiful cubic zirconia pendant.

This stunning marquise-shaped stone is a genuine cubic
zirconia—accented by an 18" gold tone necklace.
(Approximate retail value $19.95)

Send for yours today...
compliments of ✦ HARLEQUIN®

To receive your free gift, a cubic zirconia pendant, send us one original proof-of-purchase, photocopies not accepted, from the back of any Harlequin Romance®, Harlequin Presents®, Harlequin Temptation®, Harlequin Superromance®, Harlequin Intrigue®, Harlequin American Romance®, or Harlequin Historicals® title available at your favorite retail outlet, together with the Free Gift Certificate, plus a check or money order for $1.65 U.S./$2.15 CAN. (do not send cash) to cover postage and handling, payable to Harlequin Free Gift Offer. We will send you the specified gift. Allow 6 to 8 weeks for delivery. Offer good until December 31, 1997, or while quantities last. Offer valid in the U.S. and Canada only.

Free Gift Certificate

Name: _____

Address: _____

City: _____ State/Province: _____ Zip/Postal Code: _____

Mail this certificate, one proof-of-purchase and a check or money order for postage and handling to: HARLEQUIN FREE GIFT OFFER 1997. In the U.S.: 3010 Walden Avenue, P.O. Box 9071, Buffalo NY 14269-9057. In Canada: P.O. Box 604, Fort Erie, Ontario L2Z 5X3.

FREE GIFT OFFER   084-KEZ

ONE PROOF-OF-PURCHASE

To collect your fabulous FREE GIFT, a cubic zirconia pendant, you must include this original proof-of-purchase for each gift with the properly completed Free Gift Certificate.

084-KEZR